THE GA

THE GARDEN OF DELIGHTS

ROCH CARRIER

Translated by Sheila Fischman

Anansi Toronto

Cover illustration: Hieronymus Bosch *The Garden of Delights* triptych (c. 1500).

Translated with the assistance of the Canada Council, published with the assistance of the Canada Council and Ontario Arts Council.

House of Anansi Press Limited
35 Britain Street
Toronto, Canada M5A 1R7

Made in Canada

78 79 80 81 82 83 84 85 86 6 5 4 3 2 1

Canadian Cataloguing in Publication Data

Carrier, Roch, 1937 –
[Le jardin de délices. English]
The garden of delights

(Anansi fiction series; AF 38)

Translation of Le jardin des délices.
ISBN 0-88784-066-3 pa.

I. Title. II. Title: Le jardin des délices.
English.

PS8505.A535J313 C843'.5'4 C77-001722-3
PQ3919.2.C25J313

Other Anansi books by Roch Carrier
in translation by Sheila Fischman

La Guerre, Yes Sir! (1970)
Floralie, Where Are You? (1971)
Is It the Sun, Philibert? (1972)
They Won't Demolish Me! (1974)

Roch Carrier was born in 1937 in Sainte-Justine-de-Dorchester, Quebec. He holds a doctorate from the University of Paris and has taught literature for many years. He is the author of seven novels, numerous short stories, and dramatic adaptations of his novels. At present he lives in Montreal where he is a full-time writer.

Sheila Fischman was born in Moose Jaw, Saskatchewan in 1937. Her excellent translations have been widely praised by the critics, and in 1975 she won the Canada Council's Translation Award for her work on *They Won't Demolish Me! The Garden of Delights* is the fifth Carrier novel she has translated into English. She was appointed Literary Editor of the *Montreal Star* in 1978.

We dedicate *The Garden of Delights*
to the memory of
Hubert Aquin

R.C./S.F.

I

It is the time of grey pasture-lands, bare branches, of leaves chased by the wind, the season when windows are closed and the air smells of wood-smoke; it is the season of moose crucified on the hoods of triumphant cars driving back to the cities. October glides above the countryside, showing wings of autumnal red. From their mountain, the villagers can see winter in the distance. The women take warm clothes out of cedar chests, woollen blankets out of drawers. With hands reddened by the cold, the men seal chinks between windows and walls, between wood and cement. Cursing, they put shovels into the trunks of their cars. It won't be long before the roads are covered with snow. And while the women line their shelves with jars of jam the men are posted at the windows, waiting for the winter. The fields are ashen, the trees dry bones. Everything seems far away and everyone feels old. When the wind blows it leaves a bit of autumn in people's souls.

Night eats into the day, a night as dense as the black earth. When day is over the grazing lands have disappeared, and the fields and stones. Only the black night remains, and the houses and impatient children in their sweaters sinking into it. Seen from afar, the lighted windows along the side of the mountain road resemble a vein of gold in the earth of the night.

The customers in the Auberge du Bon Boire are hunched over their glasses, heads down, carefully examining the foam on their beer: they are looking for signs of the future.

"Gotta bury the past. Stick it in a deeper hole than you dig for a corpse and then shovel all the dirt and rocks from the mountain on top of it. And then have a big dance to flatten the mound! The whole parish dancing on the grave of the past! The whole country'll go crazy and dance on the past! And forget about the epitaph!"

Few people know the man who speaks, but they do know his name. Monsieur J. J. Bourdage's card has been distributed from door to door, piles of them left on the tables in the Auberge, in the taxi and on the benches in church. Monsieur J. J. Bourdage is the Vice-President of an American company. He wears a ring on every finger. When he has something important to say the sparkling hand plucks off his broad-brimmed white hat and places it on the table. His eyes fill with the silence of his reflection. Then from between teeth gleaming with gold a few words escape

"The future's going to knock at your door."

Music is being massacred at the Auberge du Bon Boire. Dancers are jigging. A small singer screams in his mother's voice.

"And are you gonna let the future in? Or do like French Canadians have always done, and lock yourselves inside like it was a polar bear?"

Monsieur J. J. Bourdage's voice is almost a shout, filled with confidence. The musicians twiddle their electric strings. The organ is like a pair of lungs about to burst. Shafts of light—red, yellow, pink and blue—fall on the dancers and each word animates their faces as a breeze rumples the surface of water. The coloured beams intersect and disperse. In the mixture of colours, sounds and night, faces disappear, leaving only the twinkling of eyes.

"To the future!"

Monsieur Bourdage raises his glass. All around him, the drinkers do the same.

"To the future that's coming on golden wheels!"

One after another they look at him.

"The carriage of the future's going to pick you up in spite of yourselves!"

Monsieur Bourdage holds his glass but does not drink. In the half-light his eyes gleam with the gold of the future.

"The main thing wrong with people today, they haven't got faith. There's no faith nowadays."

Monsieur Bourdage gets up, pushes aside chairs and

drinkers to clear a path through the mass of dancers. He jumps onto the bandstand and pushes aside the little singer, who stops his screeching. The organ falls silent, then the drums and guitars. He grabs the microphone.

"Sorry about this temporary interruption. You know who I am. It ain't that I don't like the racket the orchestra's been making, but I'm here to tell you officially: you're dancing on gold! When you get under the covers tonight you'll be sleeping on gold! There's scientific proof—just give me a few weeks and you'll have it. And while we're waiting for the future I'm buying everybody a round. Even the musicians that murder music like the English murder our language!"

Monsieur Bourdage goes back to his companions. At the microphone the little singer stammers, the organ gets back its wind, the drummer beats his drums. The hand with the glittering rings takes off the white hat and puts it on the table.

"A Heaven on earth ain't something out of the past, it's right in front of us. There's scientific proof. You have to get out of the goddamn past you're sitting in like you once sat in your mother's bellies. Today's already the past. The future's out there ahead of you, sputtering like the motor in a sports car ready to jump the first mile. The whole world's sputtering like that motor. Get rid of the past. The future's right here. You got more gold in these mountains than you got kids. Tomorrow there'll be enough gold to feed the pigs with—if that's what they like!"

He gets up. The fingers entwined with rings pick up the white hat.

"I'll be seeing you! There's scientific proof for what I said!"

At the counter he opens his cheque-book and scribbles something:

"Here's a blank cheque. Drinks on me till midnight. Whatever they want, except champagne. We'll save that for later!"

The music, softer now, follows him outside as he walks towards his white Cadillac that stands out against the night. Bourdage is humming. The moose on the roof has been bleeding and the car is streaked with blood. He turns on the windshield wipers. The Cadillac zips along the narrow winding road, swaying like a fat woman. The night is dense. Tomorrow will be fair. It's stirring like a curtain before the show begins and the earth turns its back to the night coiled around its secrets.

"Gold! Gold! Gold!" J. J. Bourdage repeats, laughing.

The night does not conceal the stones glittering in the dark fields.

The drinkers have nothing more to say now that Bourdage has left, nor have they anything to listen to. The waitress bends over them and no one even looks down her blouse.

"What can Monsieur Bourdage buy you?"

The fleshiest man indicates that she should cover the table with glasses of beer.

"You'll ruin Bourdage!"

"Don't forget though—looks like we're rich now!"

"If we ruin Bourdage it'll teach him not to throw his hay out the window and not to take himself for the Pope."

"He sure talks good."

"If a man goes to sleep with a speech like that," said Petit-Lecourt, "he won't want to wake up the next morning."

Le Gros didn't realize that he was copying Bourdage's gestures. With his fingertips he put his red hunting cap on the table before he spoke.

"To tell you the truth, I really liked listening to him talk."

"Not many guys left that still know how," said Petit-Lecourt. "With the goddamn TV, people snore better than they talk. When I was listening to Bourdage I was thinking: old-fashioned talking's come back to life."

"You swallowed all his lies."

Gros-Douillette pounded his glass on the table.

"We'd know it if we were walking on gold. Our fathers lived here before us; do you think they'd'a eaten shit three times a day if they knew there was gold around? If there was any gold they'd'a found it. They pulled out enough stumps and ploughed enough fields and dug enough wells and graves to see the goddamn gold if there was any."

"They didn't find none," Petit-Lecourt concluded. "And that proves that Bourdage's gold is a pack of lies."

"A good talker . . ."

"But no great hell as a hunter," Petit-Lecourt interrupted.

"Bourdage took his moose away just like everybody else," said a man smoking a cigar.

"Bourdage ain't even strong enough to fire a gun," Petit-Lecourt assured them.

"I seen a moose," said Gros-Douillette. "It was on the roof of his white Cadillac and the rest of you seen it too. It didn't fall out of the sky like bird-shit."

"Bourdage talks good. He didn't come here looking for no moose. Oh no! he went looking through the fields and woods and every hump of ground and all the bumps in the country."

"Just the ones on the ground," Gros-Douillette corrected him, glancing at the waitress who was carrying a tray above her head. "Bourdage don't seem to be very interested in females."

"He spent three weeks crawling over our land with his nose on the ground. And he sure wasn't hunting for his mother in the blueberry patch."

"He was looking for gold."

"He didn't find it and that's why he left."

"There ain't no gold here. What've we done to make the good Lord so happy he'd send us gold?"

"You know what's underneath the rocks here? Bedrock. If there was any gold in it we'd know about it, and there'd be more banks in the village than pigsties."

"Bourdage said we're walking on gold."

"He wouldn't'a left if he'd 'a found his fortune here; he'd'a settled down."

"Monsieur Bourdage said he'd be back."

"You believe that?"

"He ain't no hunter. He spent three weeks here and he didn't see a single goddamn moose and there's so many you have to push them together so you can see them all! I shot that moose you seen on the roof of his goddamn Cadillac." (Petit-Lecourt took off his hat and put it on the table without thinking about it, just like J. J. Bourdage.) "One day he comes and says to me: 'I'm not interested in killing, but if I don't bring back a moose people are gonna wonder what I'm doing in the woods. If you find me a moose and kill it for me I'll tell you what I'm really looking for.' I found him one, the size he wanted. That was one happy man! Bourdage was so happy he tells me, all secret like, cross your heart and hope to die, he says: 'There's so much gold here you can see it right through the rocks.' We tied the moose to the roof of his white Cadillac, he put his cheque-book against the side of the moose, a real fine animal it was, and he wrote down the amount I'd asked for the job. Then he signed it."

The cheque is in Petit-Lecourt's shirt pocket. He takes it out, unfolds it, and everyone sitting around the table can read the amount on the cheque and J. J. Bourdage's signature below it.

Just before midnight the waitress announced that it was time for Monsieur Bourdage's last round. Everyone at the table was drunk. Some time ago they'd stopped hearing the orchestra throb, affirming here, in this lost corner of the world so deep in the night, in the vast black silence, that life is an intense and vibrant dance. A few couples, drunk as well, were on the dance floor, swaying to the rhythm of their inner music. The drinkers had stopped talking. Sleeping on their chairs, they dreamed.

"I know where there's some gold," Petit-Lecourt announced.

"But you ain't gonna tell us," Gros-Douillette said reproachfully.

"There's gold in the graveyard."

Petit-Lecourt roared with laughter; he belched and coughed and choked while his companions stared at him, dumbfounded.

"It's true," Gros-Douillette conceded. "If a guy's got gold teeth he ain't got time to put them in the bank before the undertaker comes."

Petit-Lecourt wasn't laughing.

"Remember Caillouette the Notary? Remember how he didn't go to mass? They used to say he read bad books, books that changed his way of thinking. What they meant was, the Notary had some doubts about religion the way it was sold by the Curé we had in those days. They didn't have a fight. They were the only two people in the bunch of ignoramuses here that knew any Latin. Caillouette the Notary had some serious doubts about Heaven the way it was preached by Monsieur le Curé: Heaven where you turn into an angel with pretty wings and meet the good Lord face to face. And if you don't like his face you still have to look because you're condemned to Heaven. Caillouette the Notary didn't believe in that Heaven: he thought that after he was dead he'd come back to earth. Back to earth—if you ask me, it ain't worth the trouble of dying if you come back and see the same things you seen when you were alive. But Caillouette the Notary thought his soul would go on living after he was dead, but not in Heaven. Here on earth. He read that in one of his pagan books. The Notary was a little crazy. When you're dead, you're under the ground, not on top of it. But even though he was crazy he was a Notary right to the end. Apparently—and this is a confidential secret I'm telling you—the Notary said in his will that they should put enough money in his coffin to pay for a winter in Florida. So with all that money in his pockets the Notary's soul could wander around the earth pretty comfortably. That's how come I'm telling you there's gold in the graveyard—under Caillouette the Notary's tombstone. He wanted to be buried with his gold-tipped pens and his gold watch and his gold tie-clip and glasses and his wallet made out of Spanish leather full of bills guaranteed by the gold in the Queen of Canada's bank."

"If them bills were planted in a good season they'd give a hell of a good harvest!"

"Bourdage was right: we're walking on gold and we're sleeping on gold."

"On a fortune."

"Gotta go and dig it up."

"Dig it up," Gros-Douillette repeated.

Some of the drinkers had fallen asleep, heads on the table, surrounded by bottles and glasses. The others were listening to Petit-Lecourt's story, but they were too drunk to hear him.

"Yup," Petit-Lecourt repeated, "dig it up."

"Dig it up!" Gros-Douillette ordered, getting to his feet.

When they were outside the Auberge du Bon Boire, Petit-Lecourt confided to his companion.

"I heard that story from the undertaker's boy."

"You got a shovel?"

"My snow-shovel's in the car. Gotta be careful in the fall."

"I got mine too."

Petit-Lecourt and Gros-Douillette shouldered their shovels and silently walked to the graveyard beside the church. The main street was asleep and night had erased the houses. Gros-Douillette couldn't tell if his eyes were open or shut.

"Goddamn beer!"

"You see anything?"

"The graveyard."

The gate was open. They walked through the grey disorder of the tombstones. Their feet struck against mounds of earth, slipped, became tangled in the grass, which made a hissing sound.

"You sure it's here?"

"I can tell the difference between the graveyard and my vegetable patch."

"Maybe the Notary ain't here."

"The people here don't move around too much."

It seemed that the night had become paler since they'd entered the graveyard. The tombstones and crosses stood out clearly. Now they could make out the mounds of earth shaped like bodies lying under sheets. They advanced cautiously. They didn't want to fall in, sink into a decayed coffin.

"We all alone?"

Gros-Douillette recalled, like some ancient memory, the drinkers at the table in the Auberge du Bon Boire.

"Ain't the rest of them coming?"

"Two's enough when you're hunting for treasure."

Gros-Douillette was amazed that their friends weren't with them. His mind was submerged in beer. He thought the cemetery was in the Auberge, because he heard orchestra music and saw the waltzing shadows of dancers. He leaned on the handle of his shovel and thought.

"Sure gets dark at night. Hey, Petit-Lecourt! I trust you and you trust me, right?"

Petit-Lecourt wasn't paying attention to his companion's meanderings.

"It's here," he said with assurance, striking a round spot on the ground with his shovel.

Night erased the village and reigned over his spirit.

"Goddamn beer!" Gros-Douillette complained

He opened his eyes, closed them, but still saw only night.

"You see anything?"

"The graveyard."

"We all alone?"

"I hope to hell the Notary's here."

"Ask him to help us dig then. He can go at it from down below and we can take it off the top."

It's a great joke: Gros-Douillette lets out a laugh, like a cry, and the echoes of the land transmit it from graveyard to graveyard. Petit-Lecourt reprimands him.

"Try and show a little respect for the dead."

He lights a match with his thumbnail: the flame wanders across the lacework and tracery carved in the granite until a name is revealed: *Amédée Caillouette, devoted professional notary who did not wish to leave this earth.* Petit-Lecourt read only the Notary's name: he blew out the flame.

"Here it is."

"What's it say on the stone?"

"It's in Latin."

He stuck his shovel in the ground. Gros-Douillette did the same. The earth seemed hard and heavy. He wasn't laughing. A vague anxiety drained the strength from his muscles.

"You sure the Notary didn't believe in Heaven or Hell or Purgatory?"

"The Notary read in his books that after you die you stay on earth and roam."

"Roam?"

"That means coming and going."

"I don't like the idea of a dead man coming and going when I'm digging in the graveyard. Let's find another hunting ground."

Petit-Lecourt put a friendly hand on the other man's shoulder to keep him there.

"We can't run away, we're standing on top of a gold mine!"

Monsieur Bourdage's words drifted over the dense wave of night.

"You're sleeping on gold . . ."

Their feet pushed the shovels into the turf and the shovels ricocheted off pebbles and roots. Their arms tensed. The earth they dug up was as dark as the grass; it made a grating sound as it fell. Pebbles clanked. The night was so still. The cold so placid. But the earth—it seemed to be breathing. Beneath each mound was a breathing chest. A breath was hidden behind each tombstone. You could see nothing. But the night was transparent. The earth made dry, tearing sounds as they removed it. Gros-Douillette's shovel struck against something soft, without a sound.

"This goddamn night! You can't see nothing!"

They could see the boards of a coffin. The wood had decayed and become like fibrous mud. Below it was the silver cross gleaming on the lid of the coffin. Petit-Lecourt tapped it with his shovel, testing its hardness.

"We're so goddamn polite," said Gros-Douillette, "we even knock before we go inside."

Sweating, he took off his woollen shirt. Petit-Lecourt knelt at the edge of the grave. He cleared the coffin lid of earth, pebbles and accumulated debris as though removing crumbs from a tablecloth. He struck a match with his thumbnail. It burst into flame, then went out.

"You do that?"

"No," Gros-Douillette assured him, "I'm so scared I can't even breathe."

Another match cracked in Petit-Lecourt's hand: it didn't go out. He ran it over the lid of the coffin.

"Nice screws in the shape of a cross; rust-proof and shiny as new."

Gros-Douillette wanted to look somewhere else, but the stones seemed to be moving in the graveyard: walking like Sunday strollers, from one grave to another, bending down, greeting one another, kneeling. He heard them murmuring. It was intolerable: he looked down to the Notary's coffin and didn't raise his eyes. He wanted to think of something else—of the stretched-out body of the girl, breasts exposed, legs open, photographed on a leopard skin in the magazine he kept hidden under the seat of his car. He saw her picture being painted on the lid of the coffin, but the girl's ripe skin cracked and melted like a thin coating of frost. Then the bones appeared. He looked away: he didn't want to see that. Gros-Douillette's lungs were heavy as though they were filled with stones. And the wind was so cold. He put his shirt on again and stared at the little flame, which went out.

"Your knife," Petit-Lecourt demanded.

Gros-Douillette dug in his pockets, handed the knife to his companion who took great pains to open the lid: there were twenty screws, arranged in the shape of a cross, to be removed. He didn't need a match to see now. Kneeling on the coffin-lid, Petit-Lecourt soon finished the job. One to go. Done.

"You open it!" Petit-Lecourt ordered.

"No, you!" Gros-Douillette said with the same authority.

"We'll both open it!" said Petit-Lecourt, covered with sweat.

"We'll both open it!" Gros-Douillette repeated, so frightened he had stopped sweating.

Very slowly, prudently, with many precautions, trembling and feverish, completely sober, their hands gripped the edge of the coffin lid, their fingers clenched.

"One!"

"Two!"

"Three!"

"Go!"

Their muscles tensed in an effort that resembled pain. They raised the lid. In a black flash the night that covered the earth was made more silent, darker, by the night that welled out of the open coffin. Petit-Lecourt and Gross-Douillette were white phantoms in this night. Their silence was as long as a long dream.

"Anybody there?" Gros-Douillette asked finally.

Petit-Lecourt lit a match, bent down and lowered the flame.

"Is the Notary there?"

"If he went to see his girl looking like that she wouldn't know him, but I think it's him."

Gros-Douillette dared to open the eyelids.

"Looks like a rabbit that was cooked too long and stuck to the pan."

"Poor Notary," Petit-Lecourt said sadly. "All his life he thought his soul would roam across the earth after he was dead. What's that?"

A small object was shining through the rotted fabric of the Notary's suit, on the side where his heart was: a lighter. Petit-Lecourt picked it up in his fingertips. "It's like mud!" He threw away his match, pressed the lighter in different places. A flame sprang out.

"I can see his pipe!" Gros-Douillette exclaimed.

"There's a wedding ring and some other rings too!"

Gros-Douillette pointed with the edge of his shovel to some sludge that must once have been the Notary's belly.

"It's shiny there too, just over his belly-button!"

"His gold watch!"

Piously, Petit-Lecourt picked it up. He did not, however, dare to take the rings: he'd have had to touch the hands, uncross the fingers, little fingers that looked like rotten carrots.

"Get the rings!"

"Get the rings!"

"We'll get them later!"

"Ah, let him keep his jewellery!"

"Let him keep his goddamn rings!"

"If the story's true we oughtta find some money."

Petit-Lecourt thought for a while. Gros-Douillette lit up with understanding.

"In the pillow."

With rather ceremonious politeness they used their shovels to lift the hairy pumpkin that possibly remembered having once been a notary's head. In this damp place Petit-Lecourt's hand discovered a limp object which the flame of the lighter revealed to be a billfold.

"What's that? "

At the level of the Notary's hands was a box. Petit-Lecourt shone his light on the spot. A rusty metal box.

"Maybe it's his lunch-pail."

Petit-Lecourt picked it up. It was heavy.

"Poor Notary. Even that crazy religion of his didn't keep him from getting screwed just as bad as the rest of us do with ours."

At the edge of the grave illuminated by the tenacious flame that resisted the wind, the two friends stared for a while, contemplating what had become of the man.

"We do everything for him," said Gros-Douillette; "shovel him a path and even open the door, but the Notary don't want out."

"The Notary's sleeping off his death."

They tried not to be sad, they tried to laugh, but they only managed to be even sadder. They sobbed loudly as they replaced the lid of the coffin.

"Goddamn it, death's a sad thing!"

"Goddamn it, so's life!"

The lighter that Petit-Lecourt brandished at arm's length was a triumphal torch signalling the victory of two treasure hunters.

"When do we split it up?"

Suddenly remembering that he was in a forbidden place, Petit-Lecourt put out the flame. They tried to make their shadows mingle with those of the night and the tombstone.

J. J. Bourdage had trouble seeing the road. Night was falling too fast and too black over the luminous rift of the headlights of his white Cadillac; it was splattering the windshield. Often the road took a swift leap and slipped away. From time to time a little cedar house would jump in front of the Cadillac, then immediately disappear into the night. J. J. Bourdage gripped the steering-wheel, one foot on the accelerator, the other ready to slam on the brake, but his eyelids drooped and his head was as heavy as a stone in the dark water of the night. Suddenly the way was barred by a wooden fence. He slammed on the brakes and the wheels skidded across the gravel as though it were ice. His headlights shone on a wall of narrow planks, the car dived in and the wall burst. The Cadillac stopped skidding; it came to a stop. J. J. Bourdage opened his door. He heard neighing, bleating, mooing. He got out. The grass was wet. The air surprised him, like cold water on his face. He walked around his car. He'd driven off the road. He sighed. Better there than somewhere else: in a ditch, around a tree, in the bushes or upside down in a swamp. He would back up, return to the road. He got inside the car. Turned off the lights. He saw nothing now but the night. The barn he had hit melted into the night. His Cadillac dissolved in it. Above him, the stars were engulfed in the November sky. He turned off the motor. He'd sleep for a few minutes, then continue on his way. You have to take some risks in life, but not roll ridiculously off the road. He would sleep. He slumped down on the seat. You have to take risks: risk everything if there's something to gain, risk your shirt and your skin. The sweetness of this beneficient thought spread over his face and body like a caress. The leather car seat whispered, like silk and lace; an echo came to him from deep in the night, another whisper, a crackling from as far away as his childhood; the sound of sparks, the crepitation of straw under his small body. The child tried not to move in the black hole of the night. The straw crackled under the weight of his curled-up body and he thought of fire in his dark bedroom, fire as red as blood; he didn't dare turn to the curtainless window, because he would see the black night and the red fire too, and he didn't want to fall into the great hole.

The child squeezed his arms and legs tighter against his body. He hadn't eaten that night. He heard cries in his belly. He thought: there are little mice crying in my body. The straw creaked. J. J. Bourdage didn't dare to move now; the night in his arms had taken him back to the poor pallet of his childhood. He listened. Beneath him the straw breathed: a hoarse breath.

"No!"

His cry had awakened him; he sat up on the real leather seat of his white Cadillac.

"Goddamn poverty."

He started the motor. It bellowed like a bull; he goaded it on and the bull roared even louder, shaken by the inordinate beating of its large metallic heart. Fire raced through its steel veins and the bull quivered like an immense gong with each injection of the accelerator; it became turgescent in its steel skin, and rumbled and quivered and turned as though the heart of the earth itself were in that precise location. With his foot on the accelerator, a passionate foot, J. J. Bourdage made the heart of the earth beat; all around him the night was trembling. The waves furled and unfurled, spread far off into the distance and finally capsized on the other shore of night, silently; the foot continued to press the accelerator and from echo to echo, from wave to wave, the night repeated that J. J. Bourdage, in his white Cadillac, had chased away poverty; as long as the motor kept rumbling, poverty would take fright and flee. There was as much poverty in J. J. Bourdage's blood as in his white Cadillac. He wanted to shout, as fast as the motor turned:

"I'm not poor any more! I'm not poor any more!"

All the windows were open and he yelled, his voice blotting out the engine's. The night, too peaceful, contracted at his words, which shot out like cracks of a whip. His old poverty drowned in an abyss where his cries went unheard. Finally he was silent, exhausted. He turned off the motor, rolled up the windows, lay down on the seat as soft as a dream of a woman's body. The creaking of old straw had stopped now. Falling asleep was a delectable pleasure, a rich man's joy. Sleep, without thinking of morning. Wrap himself in the night . . . Beneath the dark tree bark, bugs were preparing to burst into light.

Petit-Lecourt and Gros-Douillette, arms laden with treasures, hugged the walls of the church. There was a basement vent at ground level, probably left open by the forgetful sacristan, who used it to bring the mountains of maple wood needed for heat in the winter. Petit-Lecourt examined the vent.

"If we go in there," said Gros-Douillette, "we'll be safe."

Petit-Lecourt lit the Notary's lighter and held the flame in the opening.

"We'll be safe while we split our take. Then we'll go to the Auberge."

"We'll buy a round for the house and say: Thank you, Notary!"

Petit-Lecourt put his feet inside the vent, turned around and slid into the basement on his stomach. Then he stood up. He picked up the objects he'd dropped on the ground in front of the vent. There was a smell of maple sap. A good smell. Gros-Douillette copied his motions, but because of his swelling shape it was harder for him to poke his way into the hiding-place.

"The Notary's got enough gas in his lighter to take him from Quebec City to Ottawa in a Cadillac. Round trip!"

Petit-Lecourt stuck the lighter into the dirt floor and they both knelt close to the flame.

"Let's split up our treasure."

"Fifty-fifty."

"Fair and square."

"You got the lighter; I'll let you keep it."

"And I'll give you the watch."

"How about the pipe?"

Petit-Lecourt looked at the Notary's teeth-marks on the stem.

"We'll give that to the Devil."

He snatched the billfold from Petit-Lecourt's hands.

"Let's get moving!"

Hands trembling, breathing so hard he was suffocating, Gros-Douillette unfastened the leather strap. It was putrid. His movements were convulsive. The strap broke. Petit-Lecourt observed it. Because of the shadow that stained his tense face, because of the flame that bit at the shadow as it moved, it seemed to him that Gros-Douillette's face bore some resemblance to the one he'd seen in the coffin. The flame rumpled Petit-Lecourt's face too; as he was folding back the leather flaps Gros-Douillette looked up at his companion: if Petit-Lecourt was a little more rotten, he thought, he could pass for the Notary's corpse. Anguish, like a cold hand, clawed at his back: the Notary's soul, which was roaming about the earth, might be like Petit-Lecourt. Gros-Douillette's hands were paralysed on the leather that was impregnated with death.

"Petit-Lecourt?"

"Yeah?"

"Are you Petit-Lecourt?"

Laughter stronger even than the church where they had taken refuge chased away their fear. Gros-Douillette used his thumbs to spread the lips of the billfold, which he brought closer to the flame.

"There's something better than gold in here: there's dollar bills!"

"Let's split them up."

"Not right away. Let's open the box first."

Gros-Douillette put the billfold in the little circle of light around the lighter and Petit-Lecourt slipped the metal chest inside it. How did it open? Rust had welded the lid to the groove.

"It's frozen in the rust like it was ice," said Petit-Lecourt.

"Give it here."

Gros-Douillette's big hands squeezed the metal, twisted it, tried to rip open the join. No use. It was an unbreakable shell. He put it on the ground: the mass of his body weighing on his big feet crashed down on the chest. In vain. It was as hard as a rock. He jumped again, harder.

"Don't jump so hard, you'll go right through the ground!"

The rust gave way. He lifted the lid. Something sparkled in the light. Gros-Douillette, leaning over the flame, leaned further. He read:

"Scotch Whisky."

"That's as good as gold!"

An envelope was tied to the neck of the bottle by a ribbon. Petit-Lecourt tore it off. A calling card. Lying on his stomach on the ground he deciphered handwriting that was still legible, although the ink had soaked into the cardboard:

Monsieur le Notaire, In the event that your soul goes roaming in cold climates you must not risk catching cold. From your embalmer, who wishes you bon voyage.

P. S. If there's no Heaven after death and if you're right when you say we stay on earth instead of going to Heaven or Hell, would you be kind enough to let me know? A bottle, Monsieur le Notaire, is little enough; but if you're thirsty I invite you to our place. The bar is in the corner of the room where you were embalmed. The key's behind the right front leg.

Lespérance et Fils, Graduate Embalmers.

"You think this Scotch is drinkable?"

"Scotch is like money, it gets better with time."

Petit-Lecourt unscrewed the cap and brought the bottle to his lips.

"That's what Heaven is!"

Then he brought the bottle to his lips again; the late Notary's whisky gurgled in the silence of eternity, gradually flooding Petit-Lecourt's body with an irresistibly gentle warmth. Absorbed in the events of the evening, he had forgotten that he was shivering in the damp basement on this November night. The warmth was gentle and seemed to be spreading; inside him his bones were growing like a tree, his muscles were trembling. The sap in his bones was sputtering: the ecstasy of no longer being small!

Gros-Douillette grabbed the bottle: the dazzling alcohol was turning his heart into an intoxicated bird. There was a fortune at his feet, next to a little flame that had been snatched from the other world and didn't go out. Petit Lecourt took back the bottle.

"It's even better near the bottom."

He held the bottle out to his companion, who filled his mouth, listened to the whisky singing in his throat, in his body; he closed his eyes and rested his cheek against the night.

"The bottle's empty; now we split the treasure."

They lay on the ground, close to the little flame. Gros-Douillette's big fingers pulled banknotes out of the billfold.

"I can see the zero but I can't tell if it's a ten or a twenty or a thousand."

"You can't read."

He brought the roll of bills close to the flame.

"Don't burn it!"

Gros-Douillette was filled with gratitude—a tear in his eye—to his friend for shouting. Confused by his own happiness, he'd forgotten that the fire could burn their treasure. A wave of gratitude, a wave higher than the church, rose within him and overwhelmed his soul.

"I'm glad you're my friend," he said. "I don't know what I'd do if it wasn't for you."

"They're tens; here, count them."

In the circle of yellowish light, bills were piled onto bills, new, clean, unwrinkled bills decorated with engravings from the past.

"Twenty-two . . . thirty-three, thirty-four . . . forty-four . . . There's more! There's your share and here's mine. Fifty-fifty."

"If it wasn't for you," Gros-Douillette sobbed, "I'd'a burned up my fortune." (His voice was muffled by his sobs.) "Thanks for saving me from ruin. Thank you!"

With a limp arm he held out his entire share to Petit-Lecourt, weeping.

"Thank you, my friend!"

Did Petit-Lecourt have the right to refuse this gift that God was offering him from a drunkard's hand?

Gros-Douillette got up, turned his back, crouched down and presented his behind to his friend.

"Give me a kick in the ass; when I think I could'a set fire to our fortune . . ."

"I wouldn't hurt a friend that just gave me his share."

He folded the roll of bills and placed it over his heart, in his shirt pocket.

"Right! What time is it?"

He bent over the lighter and read.

"It's three something."

"That the Notary's watch?"

Gros-Douillette recognized it. Petit-Lecourt was astonished that he had looked at this watch, and not his own, to find out the time.

"Yup, it's the Notary's watch."

"So that means it don't show the right time."

Petit-Lecourt held the watch against his ear.

"Christ, it's ticking!"

They were paralyzed, frozen as though winter had pierced them with an arrow.

"What time have you got on your watch?"

Gros-Douillette looked closely.

"Three something."

"The same time as the Notary's watch!"

"You set it."

"I didn't even wind it."

Their shadows created two strange, enormous figures on the pile of firewood. Petit-Lecourt, holding the Notary's watch, was hypnotized by the second hand, which was being pushed by an invisible finger. He couldn't hold the gold watch. It had a life of its own; it was burning; it fell from his hands with a surprising leap. Gros-Douillette picked it up. They waited, silent.

"I'm sweating off everything I drank!"

"Goddamn it I'd be scared if I was by myself."

"I'm thirsty."

"There's another bottle."

"Where?" Gros-Douillette asked, noticing that fear made his friend's voice sound strange.

"Go back in my coffin . . ."

On the pile of wood Gros-Douillette saw Petit-Lecourt's shadow, his own, and another one, very long, very thin. He wanted to yell:

"It's the Notary!"

But . . .

How had the two companions gone out through the vent? How had they crossed the village? They were drinking, sweating, drinking again, sweating, drinking to burst—and they were sitting at their table in the Auberge du Bon Boire. Petit-Lecourt announced:

"A round for everybody!"

And Gros-Douillette saw the Notary's roll of bills take flight and scatter under the ceiling, glide and slowly spin down. Everywhere, hands followed the bills, pouncing like birds of prey; everywhere, feet in big boots climbed onto chairs, jumped onto tables, knocking over bottles and glasses; everywhere, famished shouts. Already, only one bill was still flying; the rest had been picked up and the waitress put trays filled with bottles on the tables; all around them, after the shouting and laughter, silence and sleep pressed against the smoke. From a corner of the room, someone shouted:

"If you're so rich how about another shower of bills?"

Petit-Lecourt, his head on Gros-Douillette's shoulder, didn't hear. When he returned to the Auberge the fires of Hell nipped at his soul. He drank and drank, to drown them in beer. Now he was asleep. So was Gros-Douillette. But his mouth murmured:

"Treasure . . ."

"So send us a shower of gold!"

"They're trying to be like Monsieur J. J. Bourdage!" sneered the man called Arrache-Clou because his chin was shaped like the claw of a hammer.

Another drinker shook the sleeping man.

"Where'd you find it?"

He opened an eye.

"Bourdage," Petit-Lecourt stammered, "he told us we were walking on gold . . ."

"But my boots didn't touch nothing but the ground and some rocks and cow pies."

"The graveyard's full of gold," Gros-Douillette roared, still snoring.

Petit-Lecourt was startled by the roaring; his hand opened and the rings he was holding, the Notary's rings, rolled to the floor of the Auberge, where they gleamed like stars in the sky above the countryside. Arrache-Clou stepped on one with his big boots.

"It's as true as the Gospel—we're walking on gold!"

"I'm going to the graveyard."

"Wait for me, I haven't prayed for my old father for years."

"I really want to see my old aunt, the one that never slept with nobody, just her purse!"

The Auberge du Bon Boire emptied. No one was left but the Aubergiste, dazzled by the electric games of his new IBM cash-register, and the Waitress, who was looking for empty bottles in the dense cloud of smoke; later, they found Petit-Lecourt and Gros-Douillette asleep under the table.

The graveyard was on the mountain and behind it the sky was as deep as time past, or the future. The men scattered across the graveyard. They were shadows, barely visible. Their shovels gleamed.

"*Baptême*!" one of the villagers yelled. "I'm drunker than you think! The church looks as if it's all painted red."

His fear pressed down on him. His feet sank into the earth of the graveyard where the dead and the damned were crawling; he felt damp putrefied bodies slither across his legs. He screamed:

"Help! The Devil's after me!"

Eyes were torn away from the folds of black grass that probably concealed treasures, bent heads were raised up to the sky that was as dark as the earth, shovels stopped their feverish work.

"Hell's inside the church!"

Forever and ever, the church had been beside the graveyard. It was black in the night. But its windows were red. Or yellow. They were red. They shattered. From each one escaped a furious flaming devil, higher than the church, who climbed up on the walls and danced on the roof. They roared and thundered. The entire church was a huge fiery devil. The gold-hunters threw down their shovels and fled the graveyard as though the fire were burning at their backs.

"The good Lord didn't think of everything; he should'a given us hoses instead of dingdongs."

Petit-Lecourt had been elected fire chief ten years earlier. His job was to drive the fire engine and hold onto its key.

"Petit-Lecourt!"

He wasn't in the graveyard and he wasn't at home. So he must be at the Auberge! He was asleep. He was drunk. He'd sleep for two days. He'd drunk so much he'd still be drunk three days from now. They tried to waken him by kicking him in the ribs. The waitress poured a bucket of water over him. He slept. As before the creation of the world. How could he hear the cries from the mouth stuck against his ear, repeating that the church was on fire, that he had to get up because he was the fire chief? How could he remember that in his fright he'd forgotten to put out the Notary's lighter, which had set fire to the wood-shavings on the floor? The Waitress looked in his shirt pockets for the key. With a straight face she hunted in his pants pockets too.

"Hurry!" one of the women whimpered.

"If he ain't got the key I can't hatch it like an egg, Madame!"

One of the gold-hunters tried to reassure everyone:

"I'm telling you, we drank too much, we're drunk and the church isn't on fire; we see fire because we're drunk but if we weren't drunk we wouldn't see any fire!"

The waitress didn't find the key.

"I smell something burning!"

"The smoke's coming in here!"

"Church smoke in the Auberge—we can't have that!"

"Petit-Lecourt ain't got the key!"

"I'll go and see his wife."

Madame Petit-Lecourt opened the door, eyes sunk in sleep. She held her nightgown closed with both hands.

"The key for the fire engine!"

"Yes, it's here."

Arrache-Clou held out his hand. She turned her head.

"I don't lend it to just anybody."

"The church's on fire!"

"Poor Monsieur le Curé!"

"It ain't the Curé that's on fire, Madame, it's the church!"

"You'll have to ask my husband for the key, he's the one that was elected fire chief."

"Your husband won't be sobered up till the end of the month; and the fire won't wait that long."

"Who started it?"

"Somebody that don't know the difference between a vigil light and a church. Hurry up, give me the key before there's nothing left but smoke."

"The church is made of stone. Stone don't burn. I don't believe the church is on fire, I don't believe it."

Madame Petit-Lecourt turned on a light. Madame Petit-Lecourt was beautiful with her hair undone and hanging down her back. Her buttocks were broad mounds under her nightgown. If he hadn't been drunk, Arrache-Clou wouldn't have dared to put his hand on them. But he was drunk . . . and Madame Petit-Lecourt didn't protest. Waves of happiness spread through Arrache-Clou's hand.

"That's better than gold!"

"My husband keeps the key in the safe."

Arrache-Clou spread his hand across her other buttock.

"The safe's behind the door."

Madame Petit-Lecourt took her hands away from the neck of her nightgown. A treasure of a bosom glowed through the thin cloth. Between her breasts hung a small gold cross.

"Maybe you don't know it, but I'm a gold hunter!"

Arrache-Clou's other hand grazed the nightgown and came to rest on the curve of her breast.

"Here's where you should keep your treasure."

His eyes on fire, Arrache-Clou took Madame Petit-Lecourt in his arms, his hands pulling up her nightgown; they fell to the floor.

"Is the church really on fire?" Madame Petit-Lecourt sighed.

Arrache-Clou's happiness was swelling like a raging fire. But he was obsessed by the key.

"What's the combination?" he murmured.

Breathless, he lost no time: supreme happiness was racing ahead of him; he must catch it. Madame Petit-Lecourt was also dashing in pursuit of happiness, and her impatient breathing made speech difficult.

"My husband never told me."

She clutched Arrache-Clou and squeezed him against her as though by doing so she could hold back time.

"My husband's always scared somebody'll steal something from him."

The fire slashed at the roof of the church. Firebrands in the sky suggested birds from Hell. They finally managed to awaken Petit-Lecourt but he didn't remember that he had a safe.

"I'm a poor man! I ain't got a safe. Do you think I dug up a treasure?

He was so drunk that he declared he'd met Caillouette the Notary. Imagine that—the Notary, who'd been dead for years!

Hell was rumbling through the church. The assembled villagers kept their distance for fear of falling into it. The gold-hunters, shovels over their shoulders, were powerless. Other villagers came running, with sweaters over their nightshirts, in slippers and with coats thrown over pyjamas.

In the middle of the night Démeryse heard footsteps on the floor, whispers and slamming doors.

"Somebody dead?" the old woman asked. "I didn't hear any bells."

"The church is on fire!"

Démeryse ordered her bed to be pushed over to the window. Then she saw the red sky. Through the arthritic fingers of the poplar trees she caught sight of a ball of fire on the mountain where the church should have been. The church built by her father's hands. When his last hour had come, the old man told his descendants gathered around him: "I leave you my poverty and my church." Then he had died. As she would die. For everything dies.

"The good Lord can't even protect his own house."

Her father's church was perishing by fire. Her window was coloured by the large red dancing stain. Démeryse hadn't got up since Good Friday afternoon seven years before. On that day her age had overwhelmed her. It had rolled onto her like a thunderbolt. She hadn't got up again. Her legs were crushed. The very thought of getting up made her heart "sink" as she said. In her house the young people had abandoned her; she was alone, lying in the coffin of her old age, watching a fire devour the church her father had built, where she had married her three husbands, where she had held her twenty-five children over the baptismal font, where she had gone to take nine of them to the graveyard—babies and old people who were her children too. When her turn came to die there would be no more church; her funeral would take place in the fields, like the pagans! And those young good-for-nothings would gather the ashes to spread over the ploughed and planted fields because they wouldn't have time to rebuild the church before she died. She would die before the tree for the first piece of the framework had been felled. Because this was a tired century. No one did anything any more, and everyone was tired. In her father's day, people built. Démeryse's time was a time for breeding: children, cows, sheep. Give birth in the morning, roast the meat to feed twenty starving mouths at noon, cutting the meat for the smallest children with one hand, holding the newborn with the other. People didn't get tired then. There was no gold in those days—and no money either. Everything they had came from God: children, rain, the harvest. And at night her husband would fling himself on top of her like a man who had spent the winter in the bush without seeing a woman anywhere but in his male dreams. Then the church. She was filled with prayers accumulated from day to day, from Sunday to Sunday, from year to year, from mother to daughter, prayers piled up like the hay in the loft.

Now it was all on fire!

Démeryse hadn't noticed, as she grumbled in her voice like that of an unhappy old man, that she had got out of bed, put on her boots that had been in the cupboard for seven years, slipped on a coat that had been hanging on its hook for seven years—her Sunday coat. Bareheaded in the November mist, she walked to the church that was being attacked on all sides by the hundred devils of the fire. The Curé was hopelessly sprinkling drops of holy water at the flames. He was crying.

"We'll lose everything! The fire will profane even the Sacred Species!"

"Even if the fire takes everything," Démeryse thought, "it mustn't get the chalice or the ciborium or the tabernacle. They're holy. The fire mustn't get them. When my father built this church he wanted the holy treasures to be safe from everything."

She listened. Young people's voices and words. She looked. Young bodies, ill-formed. Young people from a tired time. Soft little pricks that couldn't even make a woman pregnant.

"They're young and they've got their youth to live, but I'm practically dead. I haven't got any youth to lose. So it's better to get rid of old age as fast as you can!"

She walked towards the fire, towards the church; she opened the big door she used to open when she could still go to mass, in the years of her youth. She walked into the fire. The Curé threw himself to his knees.

"Either I've seen an apparation or I saw Démeryse walk!"

Compassionate hands lifted him up; his mind and senses were befuddled by all his grief. Démeryse hadn't set foot outside for years. Démeryse was like a dead woman—people spoke about her only in the past. She was a dead woman still grumbling in her bed. Poor Monsieur le Curé! The fire in his church was making him drunker than the men coming out of the Auberge. He'd seen Démeryse walk! Paralytics walking, legless cripples running, hunchbacks suddenly straight, clubfoots untwisted, blind men seeing!

Démeryse remembered when she used to go to church. It was the only place where no one listened to her. Everywhere else, when she spoke a few words heads would turn, people would go where she told them, think as she wanted. "We women suffer enough here on earth so we know the truth and we know what's right!" When she spoke in church, God did not incline his head and Démeryse felt very small before God who resisted her and never answered her. In the silence she could discern the breathing of God. She would have liked to rest her tired head on his chest.

"You're suffering too much, Monsieur le Curé, you're seeing things."

Démeryse advanced through the cavern of fire hollowed out in the night. The rasping sound of the flames, the howling wind, the firebrands that whistled as they fell: she heard nothing. She stepped over the Lord's Table and she was inside the choir where a woman wasn't supposed to enter.

"Those gutless men won't let women inside the choir of the church. But we're the ones that have to hatch those gutless men and follow their laws! Would the good Lord rather be coddled by men or women? I'll never believe the good Lord's got that vice! No, the curés are afraid that if women get too close to the altar they'll see the curés are just as gutless as any other men. Men! They're always strong enough to climb up on a woman and stick in their little thing, but then they're scared they'll hurt their little balls. And when there's a fire, the Curé and the rest of those gutless wonders are scared they'll burn their little balls too."

Démeryse walked up to the altar.

When there's something to do they call the women. Fire was threatening the Sacred Species and Démeryse had to save them. The Curé had named Démeryse from the pulpit because she had married too often, because her husbands died too often, because she smelled of beer when she opened her mouth to take communion or because she was too old to dance with the young boys who enjoyed whirling through the music all the years contained inside her generous, warm and perfumed flesh. Youth! She was the one who made them spin! Faster than the fiddles! The gutless musicians fell asleep over their music, thinking about their women. They felt good, the young muscular bodies crushed against her, flattened against her belly and her breasts, with depraved ideas whirling around in their heads. The Curé shouted Démeryse's name from the pulpit. He pointed his finger at her, swearing that she was the devil in person in their village. People turned their heads in her direction, and the eyes in their hypocritical faces agreed with the Curé. Even the young ones! Then Démeryse got up, turned her back to the pulpit and walked out, slowly, with pride; but for a long time her perfume stayed behind. Not everyone could afford perfume from Europe. Démeryse was convinced that her old woman's body gave off an unpleasant odour, like old meat; she busied herself masking the smells of old age, covering her old body with a last breath of youth. She poured Petit Paris Fleury over her hair and rubbed her arms and legs with it and sprinkled it on her handkerchief. Démeryse's Petit Paris Fleury was famous as far as the villages on the other mountains. A young man would go into a tavern for a beer and people could tell from the scent of Petit Paris Fleury impregnating his clothes that he had danced with Démeryse.

"I'd rather smell of Petit Paris Fleury than Rotten Widow!"

It was her last fling. From his pulpit the Curé pointed his finger at her.

"She's soaked in beer. She paints her face like a fifteen-year-old. She reeks of perfume and I would have you know that the girls who sell their bodies in sordid houses on rue Saint-Paul in Quebec City use that same perfume. God told me so! What kind of death is she preparing for? And I, poor instrument of God on earth, I must absolve her of the sins of her old age that are even more sinful than the sins of her youth."

She went out, head high, eyes wet.

"You, good Lord, you kept quiet while your gutless little instrument was yelling himself hoarse. You didn't say a word. But you never pointed your finger at me either. You never told me my Petit Paris Fleury hurts your nose. You never criticized me for dancing with youngsters. God, is growing old a punishment? Is it a punishment to like young people? You never accused me of getting married too often, God. You never said a word, you just let my blood run through me as fast as a river carrying along men and youngsters and children and you never unclenched your teeth in that white beard of yours; you never criticized me or asked me for anything, but you gave me enough life to bring a whole graveyard back to life. Thank you, God. And to show my thanks I'm going to save your holy treasures. I don't want your gold to burn up in this fire along with your holy bread. I'll just ask you to lend me the key to your tabernacle because your Curé's got it in his pocket, and while your boat's been sinking, God, your Curé's taken off for dry ground. Forgive him, God, he's just a gutless man!"

There was a ceiling of flames over Démeryse's head. The

beams were contorted like suffering beasts. The altar cloth had been eaten away by burning brands. Flames fell from the ceiling but before they touched the floor they leaped out the windows. In front of the tabernacle the embers were as bright as vigil lights. In her earthly despair Démeryse spotted the small door to the tabernacle. With the key in the lock. God had taken the key from the Curé and put it into the lock of the tabernacle, the house of his treasures. There, under the soft silk, was the ciborium. She lifted the cover. It was filled with holy wafers. The gold was trickling because of the flames. Démeryse held a golden flame. A woman isn't allowed to touch these divine objects. But the gutless men would let the sacred vessels burn. The gold gleamed like fire, but it didn't burn. She lifted God's bread. She wasn't supposed to touch the holy bread.

"Forgive me, God, for saving your bread and your gold. I know my hands aren't worthy of touching such holy treasures. But if you don't like it, God, send your Curé to hold them. Remember, though, he's a man, a gutless man that's afraid of his own shadow unless he's got a woman beside him. That's the way you made them. And I like them just the way you made them! I liked them so much! Lord, give your Curé a woman; then maybe he won't be so gutless."

She found another ciborium in the tabernacle, two chalices, a lunula. It was a lot of gold to carry–she didn't have enough hands. Then there was the monstrance. She hadn't noticed it. Her old eyes, tired from seeing so much, had likely confused the monstrance with the fire. She couldn't carry so much gold.

"Give me an idea, God. When you're my age your imagination gets worn out like an old flint."

God inspired her. She took off her coat; in spite of the fire, it was very cold.

"I'll take your advice, God, but only if you protect me from the flu. It's November in our neck of the woods, and this isn't Florida. It's cold. You shouldn't go out without your coat. I wouldn't want to die from a case of flu."

She felt something warm on her shoulders. A caress. A breath of spring. God was with her. She spread her coat over the altar, piled the sacred treasures on it as though it were a sack. Her precious burden over her shoulder, she came down from the altar and crossed the nave, head high. As she walked out, the Curé in his pulpit pointed an accusing finger at her—in those days there were no burning beams on the floor—and she pushed open the big door. In the night and the smoke no one saw the outline of her shadow bent under her sack of treasures.

"I haven't got the legs I had when I was young. But if I still had legs as solid as bridges I'd be crushed here, with those gutless wonders praying to the good Lord to save his treasures all by himself."

The villagers knelt in their impotence, silent, beaten. What was the meaning of this fiery message God had sent them? Heads bent, they accused themselves of their sins. From the other side of the night the breath of God stirred up the flames that were devouring the temple. With a cry, the roof of the church swelled like a sail, it went flaming through the night and collapsed. For a moment the flames remained, clutching the night, then pounced on the debris with a flaming appetite.

"We lost Démeryse. I saw her go in but I didn't see her come out. As true as God's watching us . . ."

"Come on, Monsieur le Curé, save your tears for the real dead people."

"If Démeryse came here she'd'a come with her bed. She's stuck to her mattress."

"Démeryse is nailed to her bed like Jesus on his cross."

"But Jesus wasn't a sinner!" the Curé pointed out.

Suddenly he wept and his tears seemed black.

"Let us rejoice," he sighed, "for God is punishing us because he loves us. God puts those he loves to the test. Let us consider this trial as more precious than all the gold in the world."

Démeryse was so exhausted she could barely walk. She crawled on her knees from the kitchen to her bedroom, dragging behind her the holy treasures she had rescued from the fire. They clanked in her coat. She pushed the precious sack under her bed, then carefully propped her hands on the floor, on the braided rug; she stiffened her arms, drew herself up and managed to hoist her head onto her bed. She stretched out an arm, as heavy as though death were already holding it down, clutched the mattress and, crawling, got back into bed. It was warm. It was soft. It was so nice when her mother rocked her. She looked towards the window. Black. Closed by the opaque curtain of night.

"I thought the window was red. It was another dream. I

can't go any farther than my dreams in this gutless bed of mine."

Why was it so hard to breathe? The air tore at her throat and her lungs. She was out of breath, as though she'd been running. Run? Walk? She heard coarse laughter in the silence. Run? Walk! She was paralyzed. That's what they all said. Démeryse knew she wasn't paralyzed. She was simply worn out. Her legs were worn out, her lungs were worn out. Like old tools that had been used too much. Used too much? You can't live too much. She laughed again. She had been dreaming. How fine it is, at the end of your days, not to suffer. You can dream. She had dreamed. It was as though she'd been alive. She had dreamed that the church was in flames. The church her father had built with his own hands. She had dreamed that the men from the village, those gutless wonders, were scared as the devil of the fire. Especially the Curé. She had dreamed that she'd gone into the burning church to rescue the holy bread and the sacred gold. Dreamed. To dream is to live.

"It's late, later than it's ever been in my life!" Gros-Douillette sighed as he collapsed into bed, unable to take off his boots, which were caked with mud, with earth from the graveyard, unable to take off the checkered shirt which stuck to his skin; Gros-Douillette sank into sleep and nothing could give him the strength to resist the current, majestic as time, that carried him off to an eternity where he would exist only in his heavy breathing. Breath in. Out. Carresses to his soul.

"Where you been, road-runner?"

Madame Gros-Douillette grabbed him you-know-where; drunk, sleepy and exhausted, he had to obey. Madame Gros-Douillette pulled so hard that he felt torn apart from head to feet. It was no use moaning, crying, or putting up any resistance. He was dragged between his wife's legs.

"Call me your little golden sweetie-pie, if you can get it up."

"It's late."

"It's never too late."

Madame Gros-Douillette's hand gripped so hard that it could, all by itself, pull her husband out of the current of sleep. He sputtered in the voice of a dying man.

"Not tonight! "

"Yes, tonight. And right now! You're always bragging you got strength to spare and then some, but there's never anything for your little wife!"

Soft fat arms embraced Gros-Douillette and the desperate swell of his wife's body beneath him pleaded and offered. Her generous warmth pushed him back into the current of sleep.

"Come here!" his wife's voice ordered him from the shore, the other side of sleep.

Her energetic hand crept between their bodies.

"You're drunk right down to the end of this little thing! Come here!"

Gros-Douillette's head rolled from his wife's plump breast to her shoulder and poured a generous snore into her ear. A slap resounded, so loud that Gros-Douillette heard it and woke up.

"Are you there?" he asked, amazed.

"Where are you?"

"In the graveyard with Petit-Lecourt."

Another slap rang out.

Gros-Douillette went back to sleep; his wife's hand became more tyrannical.

"I'm gonna do it even if I have to pull your guts out of your belly!"

She pulled and pulled, pulled as you pull on the rope of a recalcitrant boat. Once again Gros-Douillette had to undergo the examination to which his wife made him submit every time he left the house. She didn't trust him—a lazy lout who feared work as other men feared the devil, a drunkard whose heart was like dry earth, a liar always talking about what he hadn't done. Had he ever thought about anything besides women? Any woman at all, as long as she had tits and a bum and the little garden where it's more fun for men to dig than in between the tomato plants. How could she know if this drinker, this liar, this degenerate had dispensed his affection to some other woman? Several years before she had had an illumination, after asking the Holy Ghost for help: every time her husband was away from the house he had to submit to an examination for fidelity when he came home. When he failed, Gros-Douillette apologized for being tired, exhausted, preoccupied: a man isn't always up to it, love is entitled to a holiday too. And in the corner of her soul where certitudes are born, Madame Gros-Douillette knew her husband had cheated, with one of those women he was always thinking about.

"You and Petit-Lecourt are like two peas in a pod—you're both lazy, drunken woman-chasers."

Gros-Douillette had been carried far, far away in a happy sleep.

"Get over here or I'll knock you down!"

His wife's command came to him like the very gentle plea of an unknown woman. He was far away, way up high in his sleep, a bird resting in the sky with outspread wings. He yelled to be heard.

"I can't right now; wait a while! We're tired because we set the church on fire."

He had shouted but he was still asleep, smiling. Suddenly he felt cold. He shuddered. He was freezing. His sleep was as damp as the church basement. He was asleep but he could see a long, narrow shadow on the wall, the same one he'd seen in the church basement. Gros-Douillette tried to find the blanket so he could hide his head. It was cold and dark in the church basement; and who was yelling, his teeth chattering?

"Don't yell so loud, Notary," Gros-Douillette mumbled, "there's people sleeping."

"Church-burner! Atheist! Communist! Anti-Christ! Fire-bug!" Madame eructed. She was carrying pots of cold water to pour on her snoring old man; she poured more water over him than the villagers had poured on the burning church. She took off the covers and threw them to the floor where they were soaking in the water; she opened his shirt and poured water on the sleeping man's skin. Then she pulled off his underpants. She inundated him. She wouldn't have yelled any louder if her house was on fire. In his dream, Gros-Douillette saw a boat slipping gently across smooth water towards an island where the palm trees from the Auberge du Bon Boire were growing; the Waitress from the Auberge was walking, holding her tray, offering her fine bosom to the sun and the shade of the palm trees. The cold water affected Gros-Douillette as his wife's hand had been unable to do.

"This is the limit!" she exclaimed.

Would she flee at the sight of the timid little animal now raising its head? She hesitated. Stopped yelling. She was silent.

"If they really set fire to the church they'll go to

jail . . . A woman's entitled to have her man one last time before he goes to jail."

Abandoning water, saucepans and nightgown, she flung herself on her husband, who was cold as ice but beginning to snore softly again. The warmth of her body was like a breeze on the island of palm trees where the girls had breasts as pretty as the Waitress's from the Auberge. One of them, noticing Gros-Douillette, sprang towards him. He let himself be taken without resisting, under a palm tree whose shadow was as soft as fresh water. Too much happiness makes words useless. And thoughts. Nothing interested him but the downy music of the beauty breathing in his ear. Between sighs the marvellous mouth murmured:

"What were you looking for in the church?"

He heard:

"What were you looking for on my island?"

The beauty's bosom caressed him as nonchalantly as the waves slapping the shore. He didn't want to keep any secrets from her.

"Petit-Lecourt and me, we were looking for GOLD."

He shouted the last word because just as the beauty was turning to fire in his arms an irresistible tide rose up in him, swelling every artery, every muscle with the force that the trees have in springtime, the force that, despite madness and despair, is responsible for the fact that there are still men on this earth. When he shouted "Gold!" his fingernails sank into the flesh of the beauty who screamed:

"Thief! Rapist! Church-burners!"

Madame Gros-Douillette grabbed his ear, the ear in which the beauty had been murmuring, and her fingers turned into lobster's claws. Gros-Douillette tried desperately to open an eye. Hell! Was his wife going to catch him with the exotic beauty? She pulled him out of bed by both ears, dragged him to his feet by both ears, made him get dressed—and by both ears she dragged him off to the presbytery.

"Criminal! You're going to confess your sins. You're going to clean your conscience!"

Madame Gros-Douillette rang the bell and rang again. The Curé had gone to bed rather late. After the dreadful catastrophe of losing his church, he had earned his sleep. His sleep was deep, but not for the same reasons as the drunken lazy husband, girl-chaser, gold-stealer and church-burner. The

Curé's responsibilities were too great: the souls of a parish were too great a burden for the frail shoulders of a man whose long studies had given him many diplomas and poor health. Madame Gros-Douillette rang again. She pounded with her woman's fist. She propped her husband against a pillar on the balcony, then she rang and waited. Where the church had stood there were red ashes. In the night, the charred and ruined beams had the sad appearance of penitents kneeling beneath the eye of God. Madame Gros-Douillette, impatient, knocked a little harder. The wall trembled; the presbytery was shaken to the roof. Some dry leaves slipped down the asphalt tiles and fell in the wind that smelled of ashes. She persisted, but the night inside remained black and silent as though everything had burned. It was an emergency; her husband had to confess his sins. Piously she turned the knob of the Curé's door. It wasn't locked. She opened it, looked for a light-switch, turned it on, came back to drag her public bandit of a husband inside by the ears, the way you drag a left-over ox to the village slaughterhouse by the horns.

They were in the waiting room. The former Curé had big brown chairs that looked like old nuns at prayer. Since then, there had been big meetings in Rome and the Church had been revolutionized. To rejuvenate the Church, the new Curé had sold his old chairs to some Americans looking for old things. He had replaced them with pretty brightly-coloured plastic ones. They were so lovely, the golden egg-shaped lamps hanging from the ceiling, and the others standing on feet as delicate as hen's feet but higher! There were stacks of French and English magazines: it looked like the dentist's waiting-room in Saint-Georges-de-Beauce. But having a sin forgiven was rather like having an aching tooth pulled out. God had promised that he would come and take the lives of all his creatures, like a thief taking gold away, by surprise; so she couldn't wait until the Curé had finished sleeping. She knew that the bedrooms were upstairs. She turned on the lights. A hallway above the stairs was illuminated. She walked up backwards, dragging by the ears her sinner, whose legs were as soft as rubber.

"Monsieur le Curé!"

First she whispered. Then she spoke, then she shouted. No reply. It was as though the Curé were away. Several doors. All closed. She knocked at the first one. No answer.

She knocked at the second. Nothing. She opened the third. The bed was empty. She propped her husband against the wall, made sure he could keep his balance.

"Monsieur le Curé!"

She pushed the fourth door open. He was there. She could hear his breathing.

"Monsieur le Curé!"

Silence. In the pale light from the hallway she could make out the shape of his body.

"Monsieur le Curé!"

Her hand was on the switch. Would she turn on the light? The soul of a church-burner was in danger. She hesitated. She was moved to pity: the poor priest must be overwhelmed with sorrow.

"Monsieur le Curé!"

Her finger pushed the switch. The Curé rose up in the dazzling light, shoulders and torso bare. She had never seen skin so white. Beside him, the breasts of a dishevelled woman sleeping with outstretched arms.

"Is that you, Monsieur le Curé?"

The priest pulled the sheet over his pale chest, but forgot to cover the bosom of the woman in his bed. The light was burning his eyes.

"Hear my husband's confession! Hear it!"

His hand rummaged on the bedside table among the bottles of pills and jars of medication. He found his rosary, tried to tell the time by it, looked again, found his watch.

"It's very late . . . It's very early!"

It was still night. It was already dawn. He saw again the flames wrapped around his church in the night, strangling it.

"Madame, it was Hell."

"Hear my husband's confession, he's the devil in person. Hear it, I beg you."

"I will forgive all his sins."

"All of them?"

"All. All must be forgiven. Because Hell really isn't very nice."

Knocking over several jars and bottles and upsetting some coins, he found his stole, brought it to his lips and put it around his neck. When he felt the silk touch his skin he remembered that he was not alone. Desperately covering himself with the blankets, he disappeared, hiding in his bed.

"I didn't see anything, Monsieur le Curé, because I know I didn't see what I saw!"

Maternally, she spread the blanket over the naked angel with dishevelled hair.

Who was the woman who dared to sleep in the presbytery, in the Curé's bedroom, in the Curé's bed? Madame Gros-Douillette lifted the blankets. With a motherly gesture she pushed back the woman's hair: it was the school-teacher, graduate specialist in catechism, Miss Catechism. She pulled back the covers.

"Monsieur le Curé, what difference does it make if a man's got all the gold from all the mines in the world if he's in a state of mortal sin? Please, hear my husband's confession!"

Under the blankets, the Curé was trembling. Madame Gros-Douillette stroked the night-capped head and the priest stammered:

"It's your husband who should hear mine!"

The Curé kept his eyes shut to avoid seeing the red glare of the fire that refused to die. Although the church was destroyed now, it still blazed, with great gasps. Fire fed on fire, flames devoured flames. The strong wind tried hard to keep the red light glowing until the imminent arrival of dawn. The flames pursued the last bits of debris. In its stomach the fire ruminated the last mouthfuls of the disaster. How could he sleep? Visions of red scratched at his eyes and he wept. He waited for day in the hope of a sign from Heaven, like the captain at the helm of his ship lost in a sea of fire. The presbytery was wrapped in a whitish foam. He walked from window to window. They were all submerged. The wind stirred up smoke from the still smouldering ashes and the fog that rose from the earth. The day that would follow the night was already advancing. Someone rang the bell. The Curé opened the door. The eyes he saw were so beautiful that fire and smoke were wiped out.

"Come in quickly, my child. Ah! this cold!"

Her coat was wet at the shoulders, as though she had been walking in the rain. Her hair too.

"Forgive me for disturbing you so late but this disaster is turning all the laws of propriety upside down."

She raised her head to receive the Curé's reply. What a fragrance! In the effluvia of charred wood and stones he thought of apple blossoms. Had she been crying? Her eyes were ringed with sorrow. Her big eyes . . .

"The pastor's house is always open to his flock."

Her eyes were green beneath unruly wisps of hair. The Curé had never noticed the eyes of the catechism teacher before. He smiled as he recalled the villagers' sense of humour that had named her Miss Catechism. He could hear her breathing. Miss Catechism's body was nothing but her breathing, under her coat. The Curé walked to the window.

"Monsieur le Curé, is the fire that destroyed our church a sign that God wants his entire Church, built by Peter, to crumble and disappear? You know, Monsieur le Curé, that the church is a ship obedient to all the winds. There are no more faithful now, no priests, no sin. Monsieur le Curé, what is left of the true Church of Christ? Ashes, only ashes that smell of the past."

The Curé tore himself away from his contemplation of the blazing debris and came over to Miss Catechism, who was looking up at him, large eyes open to receive the light she asked of him, lips seeking some quenching water. He approached her. She waited. He must speak. He closed his eyes and folded his hands. He heard her breathing.

"The rock of our church has crumbled, the wood of our church has burned, but our priests have not been destroyed."

Two small, burning, frightened hands clutched his folded hands.

"But nothing on earth happens without God's consent."

"That is what we must believe, my child."

The Curé would have liked to cross his hands on his chest but he couldn't pull them away from hers, so small and strong.

"So it was God who from time immemorial has decided to burn down the church our grandfathers built for Him."

The Curé didn't dare open his eyes because in the depths of his soul he knew that he couldn't look at her dazzling expression of anguish without feeling dizzy. His breath covered the young woman's. The small hands slipped away. The Curé turned his back, opened his eyes and walked to the window. A very tall flame burst through the smoke, then fell and drowned in it.

"God has allowed his temple to be destroyed," he said at last. "He wants his church to be reborn from its ashes. He wants our village church to be reborn from the ashes of our grandfathers' past. God wants a modern church, because God has always been modern. And it will remain modern, for eternity."

The young woman threw herself to her knees, arms outstretched.

"Monsieur le Curé! Monsieur le Curé! When I'm an old woman I'll remember what you've just told me. When I'm sitting on the edge of my grave your words will still comfort me."

She took a dainty handkerchief from the pocket of her coat and offered it to the Curé. He accepted it. With diligent fingers she unknotted it. Lifting the corners one at a time, religiously, she revealed rings, earrings, chains, necklaces.

"I want to be the first to participate in the rebirth of the Catholic Church, modern and eternal!"

The jewels in the Curé's hand sparkled like a great treasure too heavy for a single man to hold. He staggered and his head dropped onto Miss Catechism's hair. She burst into tears of joy.

J. J. Bourdage was asleep and the night belonged to him.

But the first light of dawn fell on his white Cadillac like a sledge-hammer pounding on his windshield. He sat up. The door was open. Policemen all around, holding guns. Big hands dragged him out of the Cadillac, clutching his clothes and hoisting him to his feet. There was a gun at his neck. They took away his watch, stripped him of his rings, the chain around his neck; they emptied his pockets, grabbed his billfold, cigarette case, cufflinks, gold lighter, bracelet. They pushed him into the police car. He was not allowed to turn around to look at his white Cadillac. He was silent. Like a poor man.

"Monsieur le Curé, you're a priest and you have to hear my husband's confession!"

Bewildered, the priest agreed. Madame Gros-Douillette ran to drag her husband away from the wall that kept him from sinking to the floor. She brought him to the priest and he fell to his knees.

"Okay if I sit down? The damn walls in here chase after you so fast it makes me dizzy."

At a sign from the priest, Madame Gros-Douillette made her husband sit down.

"Now my son, what sins have you committed?"

At another sign she left the room and, with religious circumspection, closed the door.

"My son, your wife tells me you have offended God."

"Father, I confess to the sin of treasure and the sin of fire."

"Despite the light of God, my son, I don't know what you're talking about."

"Father, I confess to setting fire to your church."

"Fire, my son? Did you say fire?"

The Curé rose up, astonished, clasping his hands towards Heaven in an imploring gesture, not realizing that under the sacramental stole he was naked.

"My son, did you really set fire to the church?"

Gros-Douillette opened his eyes. The Curé was facing him. Funny, he seemed to be naked. Gros-Douillette rubbed his eyes. He could see two curés: one, two. Two curés who were moving: one, two. One curé looked like the Curé and the other one didn't: he looked like Miss Catechism. Both curés seemed to be naked, which was funny, very funny! He closed his eyes. He thought he dreamed that the two curés were weeping copiously. Their sorrow made him sad; he would cry along with them. A cold hand clutched at his neck.

"Dammit, did you set fire to the church?"

Gros-Douillette opened one eye. Feet were kicking him. His back, his stomach. And there was shouting. The two curés, the one who looked like the Curé and the one who looked like Miss Catechism, were dancing around him, flailing and hitting and threatening and flogging: two naked devils hitting him so hard that Gros-Douillette was sorry he'd agreed to open the gates of Hell by opening the Notary's coffin.

"Why did you burn down the church? Cursed man, why did you toast God's holy bread? Why did you destroy the golden tabernacle? The golden chalice? The golden ciborium? The golden monstrance?"

"Punishment! Penitence! Whips! Torture!"

"Why did you roast the body of Christ on his cross?"

Gros-Douillette, shaken, dazed, prostrate, unclenched his lips.

"Good Lord, have pity on your black sheep."

The words slipped from his mouth with tremendous pain, the suffering inflicted by a great tearing, like the one of birth. And the pain slowly dissolved like a cry that echoes and diminishes.

Gros-Douillette thought he saw the flames of Hell around him: so many flames! More than the ones that devoured the church. Now they were still, silent. The only fire came from an electric light under a shade. The Curé's face, close to him, was wet with tears.

"My son, God cannot forgive your hardened soul that refuses to cry."

"If you really want to know, it wasn't me that set fire to your church; it was Caillouette the Notary. He was pissed off at Petit-Lecourt and me for stealing the Scotch and the treasures out of his grave."

"My son, we must wrench the sin from you as the flesh is scraped away to clean the bone. It is God's will."

God is a loving heart. God is good bread. If God really sees everything how could he be angry at Gros-Douillette and Petit-Lecourt? He saw the scene with the eyes of the good Lord that see everything, even a speck of dust hidden under a pebble at the bottom of the sea in the dark. God saw that Gros-Douillette and Petit-Lecourt had only lit a little flame, the one in the Notary's gold lighter, a flame hardly bigger than a spark. God would forgive them, otherwise he wouldn't have created fire! After all, what's the sun? Fire. And God put nearly all his might into that fire. So how could he criticize Gros-Douillette or Petit-Lecourt for striking a flame, one tiny little flame, a teeny weeny flame, when He, the good Lord, had set the whole universe ablaze one night?

"So I'm just confessing to the sin of treasure."

"God won't allow me to forgive you!"

A shout, a woman's shout, stabbed Gros-Douillette in the back. A woman burst into the room. It was his wife—he recognized her.

"Monsieur le Curé, I swear I wasn't listening but I guessed that you don't want to forgive my husband. But if he's going to lie in the fires of Hell Monsieur le Curé, where am I, his wife, going to lie?

She moaned as though the Devil's claws were already pricking holes in her quivering mass of flesh.

Miss Catechism had taken refuge in the cupboard, among the soutanes that smelled of incense and tobacco. As it wasn't appropriate for a young woman to be naked in the Curé's bedroom, she took a soutane off a hanger and put it on, hands trembling over the buttons which she inserted piously into the row of buttonholes on the holy garment.

"Forgive him!" Madame Gros-Douillette implored.

Her husband noticed that the Curé had gone outside. The night was black. Black as his incendiary soul. Black as Gros-Douillette's soul. Black as his hands in the night of the church basement. From now on, to the villagers, his skin would be blacker than a nigger's. His skin would be so black the day would no longer exist for him. In his shame, even the light would be black. Around his chest, the night fell as heavy as the earth drawing in around him. Ah! Gros-Douillette would never again set foot in the Auberge du Bon Boire. Never again drown his thoughts in beer. He would swear on his mother's head to stay as dry as a summer without rain. He'd drunk too much: the first few bottles release laughter that's hidden in holes like groundhogs, but if he kept on drinking, terror would spring out, terror hidden deeper than any groundhog, and remorse and regret and fear. They would crawl around him as though the earth itself had turned upside down, with all the teeming slippery life that crawls beneath the flowers and green grass. He'd never drink again. A night as black as this is what a corpse sees in his coffin, like the one Caillouette the Notary was seeing before Gros-Douillette and Petit-Lecourt opened the door to the real night, the one with stars blazing in it, and angels skating across the blue sky. He'd never drink again.

The church was before him, still standing. It had never burned. He walked towards the big wooden door decorated with cast ironwork and screws. He pushed at it with his shoulder. The hinges creaked. The smell of candles and prayers: the smell of the good Lord. He had dreamed the other day that the church was blazing like a match. A crazy dream. The night closed in on him like a creaking door. He could make out the steps of a black staircase. The staircase that went up to the organ. His feet groped for the steps. He'd never seen the organ. He had heard its voice since he was a child. And the nave was quivering like a vast bosom. The organ was up there. The steps were soft. Gros-Douillette was a little drunk but he'd never drink again. Set fire to the church . . . fire . . . He didn't dare light a match so he swam through the night with broad flabby motions.

Far away in his soul, the prickle of a feeling of gratitude to the good Lord, too good, was born. It grew and surrounded Gros-Douillette and spread even further; the whole night was filled with the gratitude of a humble creature to his God. Gros-Douillette's hands came crashing down on the keyboard, releasing seething notes. The fragile night would crumble to ashes beneath the oncoming light of morning. He wanted to give thanks but his voice wasn't powerful enough to be heard by his distant God. He would borrow the voice of the organ then. Gros-Douillette shouted:

"Thank you, God, thank you!"

It wasn't enough. It was only the small cries of a man, lost in the sea of the night like grains of sand.

"Thank you, God! Thank you!"

His hands raced over the keyboards, pushed and pulled on the stops; his feet danced over the pedals. A great wind, a powerful gust, a storm rose: the night trembled, enormously black, swollen by the wind he had unleashed.

"Thank you God!"

His clenched fingers held onto the sunken keys of the great organ, his feet stamped furiously on the pedals and made the pipes tremble; he couldn't open his mouth wide enough to let out the powerful cry stirred up by the bellowing of a hurricane; the pipes would burst and suddenly Gros-Douillette's great cry of gratitude to his God would spurt out in flames at the ends of the pipes; birds of fire, they would fly away. Gros-Douillette pounded at the keyboard, possessed by the frantic desire to make the night of Heaven melt like frost at a window. The breath of the organ was the breath from his own lungs. The organ wept and howled, it released cries of fire.

Gros-Douillette thought he heard his own voice.

Under the violent action of his feet on the pedals, the earth dropped out of the night, and all its outstretched fibres cracked. Slowly the night was pulled out of the earth; all the roots of the night twisted and struggled and the fire swelling from the organ spread into a shower, a torrent, a shining river that carried away Gros-Douillette.

Late that morning Démeryse's family realized that she wasn't asleep: she was dead. Later still, her daughter noticed Démeryse's coat folded under her bed. Who could have taken the coat out of the closet and stuck it under there? She picked it up. A sound of metal: chalice, ciborium, lunula, monstrance, hosts—the holy treasures tumbled to the floor.

"Help!"

The family came running, dry-eyed, because Démeryse was so old, so sick, that her death was a deliverance. The church treasures! Their eyes filled with tears. They would have been no more surprised if they'd seen from Démeryse's window the church itself, still intact. They called the Curé. He arrived out of breath, giving his benediction, pale as a soul from the graveyard.

"I saw Madame Démeryse go into the burning church," the Curé repeated. "I stated so publicly. I saw Démeryse walk into the fire as though she was walking through a door. Unfortunately, these days when gold and silver are gods, parishioners won't believe their pastor."

"Come on, Monsieur le Curé, it's impossible. Démeryse couldn't use her legs. They were like butter. God had taken away her muscles and her bones."

"Démeryse's body was half dead."

"Then it was her soul, her immortal soul, that went and saved our treasures. God wanted Démeryse, the weakest of all of us, to rise like the lame man in the Gospels and save the sacred gold from the devastating flames, because gold is God's own metal."

The Curé knelt before the precious objects, miraculously saved. With the respect due to mysteries, to miracles and to gold, his lips grazed the treasures.

"I don't understand. Did the Devil come and take the ciborium and Démeryse at the same time?"

"If you ask me, it's a miracle: Démeryse hasn't walked for seven years. All of a sudden she walks—and then she dies!"

They spoke of the miracle in neighbouring villages where only the young children didn't know Démeryse; they wrote about the miracle in the *Journal des Catholiques*, which was published in Quebec City; they talked about Démeryse's exploits on television—even on the English television in Montreal. People flocked to her coffin. Many of them had danced with Démeryse, held their arms around her thick waist and her hard-skinned bosom that was as warm as the sun. All prostrated themselves before Démeryse. Even their wives were moved. Démeryse was sleeping in heavenly peace, in the light from the holy treasures she had saved. The candles, flames multiplied by the convex gold of the precious vessels, surrounded Démeryse with an aureola that was not of this earth.

The next morning, when Petit-Lecourt's memory resurfaced, he confessed to his wife that he'd set fire to the church. She didn't hit him. She listened without roaring or clawing. She listened, without seeming to believe it, to her husband's account of every stage of his adventure, his discovery of the treasure and the episodes that followed. She didn't yell. She didn't strike out. She didn't cry. He insisted that he hadn't set fire to the church himself; he had seen with own eyes, seen "as clear as I can see you," Caillouette the Notary spreading the fire through the church basement, like butter on bread.

"You all done?" she asked, almost gently.

"If I told you anything else, it'd be a lie."

She didn't jump on him. Slowly, she opened the door.

"Arthur!" she called.

A big dog came in, mud clinging to the hairs on its paws. It wasn't a pugnacious dog: she had named him after a man who didn't want to go to war. She only let him out on a chain. She unfastened the chain from his collar and without striking or insulting her husband, she attached the chain to the belt around his trousers. Then she fastened the chain. Somewhat amused, somewhat disturbed, Petit-Lecourt watched her search in the cupboard. A padlock. She inserted the ring of the padlock in two links of the chain, slipped the key between her breasts and pushed her husband outside.

"If I let you run around you're going to make more trouble than your dog. Arthur never set fire to the church. And when he digs up bones it's because he's looking for bones. If he was looking for gold, he'd find it."

While his dog frisked around, free and dirty, Petit-Lecourt watched the approach of winter from the end of a chain.

"Poor Gros-Douillette."

II

Underfoot, the ground was growing hard; already, there was ice hiding in it. If you left the road to walk on the grass you could hear sharp crackling sounds that weren't made by the wings of frightened insects, as in summertime, but by something breaking. The sky was getting lower, coming closer every day.

"It's heavy. Loaded down with snow."

"Getting ready to pop."

Soon the belly of the sky would open for the birth of winter.

At the Auberge du Bon Boire, though, there was warmth! The villagers, back from hunting, waited for the first snow.

"Winter again."

"If we were rich we'd never have to see it."

"We'd buy ourselves a little piece of land under a sunbeam!"

"If we weren't so poor."

Words that had been said and said again drifted through the smoke from pipes and cigarettes.

"They say there's gold underneath our feet."

They were silent. As though the man with the white Cadillac had sat down at their table. They were silent, listening to his words echo through time.

"Dig, dig! There's gold. There's scientific proof!"

"Gold around here, with our cows starving to death? Can't be."

"The golden carriage of the future will carry you away whether you want it or not."

The man with the white Cadillac was speaking. Under the mountain, in the fields, under the ploughed furrows, under the frozen ground, there's as much gold as there was snow last year. The villagers reflected. When they left the Auberge the wind raced before them like a wild horse, trampling their pleasure.

Soon the snow fell on the ashes of the church and on the grey stubble. It fell on the roofs and on the fields. Snow covered the road that went through the other side of the forest to the villages below. All was silent, all was white. The snow concealed the road, blurred the neighbouring villages, erased the black debris of the church. In the graveyard, the tombs of Gros-Douillette, whose body had not been found, and of Démeryse and the Notary, disappeared under the snow like things slipping into oblivion.

Everyone became a little deaf, muffled in their dreams. In houses heated by electricity there was a sweet nostalgia for the wood that used to spread its fragrance, its crackling and its songs from the fire in the stove. The cold came in through all the cracks. Hoar-frost stuck to the windows, which gradually closed their eyes on a white silence. The cold slept on people's lips. Words turned cold on the tongue. Between sentences, speakers would dream. The bark on the trees turned as hard as the villagers' skin. They dreamed of summer. They dreamed of fall. The snow wiped out the present. They remembered past winters like this one, when everyone had waited for spring. The past lay in wait under the snow. The villagers spoke of other snows, those of yesteryear when storms had frightened the men and made the women cry, when storms had swallowed up the villages in their white eddies. These stories were told with the trust of old sailors repeating tales of past shipwrecks with waves that grow in fierce intensity from telling to telling. Then they were silent. Listening. In the silence the stories went on, voicelessly repeating themselves. And so the villagers, muffled in the fur of silence, listened to names that were repeated like the memory of another time.

There were five or six. They rocked and knit and dozed and smoked and sewed. Piously, they stirred up the fire of words. They had gathered in the house of the New Notary, who had succeeded Caillouette the Notary after his death.

Madame Petit-Lecourt and her dog, Arthur, were living in the house while the Notary escaped the winter on the beaches of Florida.

"A house needs somebody in it, especially in the winter," Madame Petit-Lecourt had said in the doctor's waiting-room. "But I need other bodies around me too; I get bored in this castle where the halls are bigger than my whole house. The new Notary told me, he said, 'Make yourself at home'; and when I'm at home I invite people over."

And so the villagers gained access to Caillouette the Notary's castle. Petit-Lecourt was responsible for protecting his own house, but he was forbidden to go any farther than his chain.

The soul of Caillouette the Notary had come to join their conversation. The Shoemaker remembered. The Shoemaker told the story as though it were the first time:

"All of a sudden what do I see standing right there on my floor, with his feet in my scraps of leather? The Notary! I tell you, I was surprised, because with those shiny little shoes of his and his starched cuffs and his big city suit, he'd never set foot in my shop. No sir. He'd'a got dirty walking through the oiled harness hanging from the ceiling, or in between the collars and the ropes and the saddles and the greased traces and the jars of black polish. He could'a got dirty just shaking my hand. Likely that's why he didn't do it. So there I am, standing with my hand sticking out in the air. My hand looked pretty stupid, like a horse that's been hanging around with his mouth open for two days, waiting for his feed. The Notary, he's holding two shoes in his little white hands and he puts them down on my counter. His hands were as white as an embroidered tablecloth that's been wrapped up in blue tissue paper and never seen the light of day. Clean white fingernails. Hands that never done a lick of work. I can still hear his little voice, as high as the last note on the harmonium: 'Make me some thick soles, as thick as that, more than two fingers, but hollow inside, yes, that's right, a kind of little trough inside the soles.' Those shoes had never touched the ground we walk on, fine black shiny shoes they were. 'They're my burial shoes. Make me some thick soles with a little trough inside. Understand?' So after I cut out the soles and hollowed out his little troughs I let the Notary know, like he asked me to. That was when I saw those little fingers of his take a wad of bills, more than there is in the bank in Saint-Camille-de-Bellechasse, and stuff them inside the soles of his shoes that were as thick as a fresh apple pie. Then I put the last leather sole on top of the little troughs full of money, stuck in my awl and sewed them up. He took the shoes and he paid me. I can still hear that little voice of his that didn't talk loud enough to move a speck of dust: 'This is a secret between you and me.' Then he left the shop, but he came back a little while after. 'If that secret leaves your mouth just once I promise you I'll get out of my coffin in my nice burial shoes and I'll get in your bed in between you and your wife. When you reach out for her you'll be touching my body. My cold dead body, because you've betrayed it.' I can still hear him. 'I want you to be silent. This is an oath.' I can still see him. And when I tell you all that, I wonder if maybe the Notary's in here with us, listening to me, hiding in the smoke from my pipe. I been keeping his secret on the side of the room there, where you put things you want to forget. I didn't tell it till a whole winter after my late wife was dead and buried."

"That was when the Notary started going crazy."

"Crazy? He started going crazy way before then."

"Maybe he wasn't crazy and the rest of us are."

"Can I get a word in?" a woman asked. "This is a good one."

Imelda Boucher used to make the suits for all the men in the village before it was fashionable to look like sissies.

"Damn silly fashions! A man always puts the same thing inside his pants, so why does he want them to be skin-tight in June and baggy in November? In the days of Caillouette the Notary . . ."

Even the Notary used to ask Imelda Boucher to make his suits. A single privilege set him apart from her other faithful customers: he bought his own cloth from an Italian in Montreal.

"I can't talk," Imelda Boucher insisted. "As long as my Thomas is still alive I can't talk. My lips are sealed. And my Thomas is as healthy as a horse. Thomas, he's got a pair of lungs as solid as the bridge in Quebec. His own father was ninety-five when he died. And his mother died fifteen years later, when she was ninety-nine. I'm not going to be talking tomorrow."

Imelda Boucher got up as though to put a log on the

fire, but remembering that the fire ate electricity now, she sat down again.

"I'm not supposed to talk," she said, "because I swore an oath, but everybody knows you put shoulder-pads in the jackets. In those days it was the style for men to have a head on their shoulders that looked like a jug on top of an ice-box. And I knew something most people didn't know: the Notary had one shoulder lower than the other one. As if he'd been carrying water all his life! Poor Notary: he didn't have any chest. The skin on his chest stuck to his back. It's true, you know, if you spend your whole life bending over wills and money you don't get a chest like Mr. Universe. But the Notary was vain, like a turkey. He always used to ask me to make him shoulders and a chest. So I'd take two pieces of this cloth that you put in the linings and I'd put in padding, lots and lots of padding, so when the Notary wore his suit he had the shoulders and the chest he should'a had. The Notary was a steady customer. Oh, he cheated on me a few times—he bought some suits in Quebec City and Montreal and even farther away when he went there. But I can say in front of everybody that when the Notary wanted to get himself a suit to be buried in he came to me, Imelda Boucher and nobody else. I can still see him standing there in his green-and-yellow striped undershorts, with those big English shoes on his feet and his socks and his legs like pencils and his little chest with the bones sticking through the meat like fish-bones. I remember his little belly too: he spent so much time hunched over his papers that all the skin on his body fell down to his knees. All of a sudden, the Notary looks me in the eyes. I say looks but it was more than that. His eyes were like nails that went right through me. Nailed to my chair. I can still hear his little voice, like a cough, begging me: 'For my burial suit I want you to give me a torso and shoulders and biceps like the Montreal Canadiens. When I'm dead I want to be what I haven't been while I've been alive.' 'Monsieur le Notaire,' I tell him, 'if you want biceps and shoulders and a chest like that I'll have to put in an awful lot of padding, or maybe feathers, like a pillow.' 'No,' he says, as mad as if I'd said his mother was some kind of animal, 'No! Here's what you're going to use.' Then he opens up his briefcase and he shows me what he brought to stuff his burial suit with."

"What was it?"

"I can't tell you. If I told you one iota—last Sunday the Curé explained how big that is, an iota—of what I saw in his briefcase, my Thomas he'd have an explosion in his heart as soon as I said the word. But I'll swear on a stack of Bibles that what I saw, there was enough of it to furnish a new church. But you won't make me talk. I swore the Notary an oath I'd be as silent as the grave."

Imelda Boucher had told her story in all the houses in the village. When the sky grew dark Imelda remembered the Notary, and then she would tell her story. When the wind blew through the bare autumn branches she thought of the Notary's soul and she would tell her story. In the winter, when the wind was sharpening itself against the hard stones of the snow, it whispered the Notary's name and Imelda would tell her story. Never did she say, though, and never would she, as long as her husband Thomas was alive, what she had used to pad the Notary's suit. The others rocked and knitted, smoked and dreamed.

"Too much money!" Aristote Fait-Toute, the carpenter, tossed his observation into the silence that followed the end of the story. "Too much money! That was the seed of his craziness."

"Crazy!" Madame Petit-Lecourt was surprised.

From the cupboard she took down a cup with a floral motif hand-painted by the wife of Caillouette the Notary, poured herself some tea, went back to her chair, took a sip and started rocking again.

"Crazy?" she repeated, "The Notary wasn't crazy."

"When a man wants special soles on the shoes he's going to wear when he's dead," said the Shoemaker, "it's because he's caught a cold in his brain. You can't tell me any different!"

"When a man asks the best seamstress in the township to put a little extra something inside the suit he's going to wear when he's dead," said Imelda Boucher, "it doesn't matter how high he holds his head when he walks down main street, you can't help thinking he's got frost on the brain."

"Caillouette the Notary wasn't crazy," Madame Petit-Lecourt broke in, her chair still now. "I know what I'm talking about. When a woman's washed a man's floors and his shirts and his dishes and his socks and his sheets for years, she knows a lot about that man. The Notary wasn't crazy. I knew that man better than his own wife did, because Madame la

Notairesse didn't wash his socks or his sheets or his dishes. How do you expect a man to love a woman that turns up her nose at his socks? I know there was no love lost between those two. Love never entered their hearts. All the love he could'a given his wife he gave to his money."

"It don't bother me," said Aristote Fait-Toute, "to say right here in front of everybody that the Notary was as crazy as a dog with a hornet on his ass. Sure he was crazy, but around here you don't lock up a crazy man that can talk Latin."

"Is it crazy to think about the kind of life you're gonna live after you're dead?" asked Madame Petit-Lecourt.

"Sure it is, because that's something you can't know about. You can try and see what's ahead, on the other side of the window, but there's always some frost in your way. A man can scrape away at it all his life, but that frost'll always be there. Scrape if you want, wear out your fingernails up to the elbows, but you'll see. That's why it's crazy to think."

Aristote Fait-Toute's big fingers closed around his plastic tobacco pouch, an unsuccessful imitation of the ones people used to make from pigs' bladders. Everyone fell silent again.

"If a man knows how to plant money and bank up the dirt around it and water it and protect it from bugs so it bears fruit, is that man crazy? When it was your money the Notary turned into flowers did you call him crazy then? The Notary was a genius!"

"A genius that crossed the bridge of madness," Aristote concluded.

"Tell us about the ceiling there," Madame Petit-Lecourt interrupted.

"The ceiling? Bare baby Jesus! The ceiling!" Aristote repeated. "Every house has got a ceiling! It's a common thing, a ceiling. And if somebody's got a hole in their ceiling then they're crazy like the Notary. It's just that they didn't put him in a strait-jacket because he could talk English and Latin."

"And Greek too, as far as I could tell," The Postman's Widow insinuated.

"Maybe the crows in the village talk them languages!"

"And the Curé!"

Aristote Fait-Toute emptied his pipe by knocking it against his palm.

"I ain't supposed to talk about the Notary's ceiling. It's a secret. If I let one word about it slip onto my tongue I'll be poisoned by my own spit. The Notary prophesized it."

Aristote Fait-Toute stuffed his pipe with fresh tobacco, looked for a match and waited until all ears were listening to him, all eyes pretending to be bored.

"You know, Aristote, you got a hell of a good resistance to poison! There ain't a soul in the township that hasn't heard the story about the ceiling three times over!"

"It's a secret between me and the Notary and my lips are sealed. It was a secret under oath, as secret as what colour panties the Curé's housekeeper wears. The Notary asked me to make him a new ceiling in his dining room. Bare baby Jesus, it's normal to ask a master carpenter when you want a ceiling!"

Aristote Fait-Toute was hidden in a cloud of smoke.

"You can pull all my nails out and burn me with a branding iron and cut off the parts of me that aren't Catholic. I still won't talk."

Once again silence reigned in the kitchen, as it did outside, in the snow. Backs were arched. The silence must end.

"You and me," said Imelda Boucher, "we come from the same village, the same past, practically the same mother and father. So if we talk about the things we know it's the same as if you were thinking about them all alone inside your heads."

"My mother often said 'Trading secrets isn't breaking them.' "

"If Aristote tells us about the ceiling I'll tell you about the Notary's pillow!"

Aristote inhaled a puff of smoke that went right down to his stomach and climbed back up to his thoughts, which became muddled.

"What if the Notary comes back?"

"Send him over to see me," said the Widow Gros-Douillette. "He sure wouldn't go and see his wife. I'll show him a real widow!"

"I'll tell you everything about the ceiling."

Aristote spat to clear his voice. He was about to begin his story. He had already prepared the first sentence. He took a breath before starting, but Imelda Boucher, the Seamstress, spoke first.

"I give you my word as a woman, but if I accidentally break my oath I hope you'll understand it wasn't out of spite."

"The body of my ghost will come into your bed if you don't respect our secret."

"You think my husband'll let you get away with that?"

The Notary unrolled the silk as carefully as he opened his papers.

"You're going to make me a small pillow. A very special one. I want lace all around it and I want my initials embroidered on the corners. And I want it soft, because I'll be sleeping on it for a long time."

"The Notary smiled then. I'll remember that smile for a long time. I can still see it. It wasn't just his mouth that was smiling, it was more like a smile on a man that was already on the other side of his grave."

"I'll make you a pillow as soft as a cloud, with little yellow baby chick feathers inside it."

"No! said the Notary. "Not even the down of a week-old chick."

"Did you think of telling him you'd stuff it with the hair off your bum?" asked the Shoemaker.

The men drew on their pipes; the chairs rocked faster, the women speeded up their knitting and darning. They had to hold back, because laughter would disturb the train of the story.

"I made him a lovely pillow, with lace and embroidery and hemstitching and French knots. It was pretty enough to put in a frame and hang up in the church. The Notary came back. He didn't say anything about the pillow but he smiled from ear to ear. Not one word, but he opened up his little suitcase right in front of my eyes.

"I asked him if that was the stuffing for the pillow and he answered me by picking up a handful of what was inside the suitcase."

"I don't suppose," Aristote Fait-Toute insinuated, "that it was full of sh . . ."

The men drew on their pipes, the women's needles, wool and thread raced.

"I didn't give you any of my currant wine," said the Widow Gros-Douillette. "My husband picked the currants just before he died. I didn't dare make wine, you understand, because I was a widow in mourning. But I figured that just because Gros-Douillette was rotting I didn't have the right to let those currants rot too, currants he'd picked with his own hands. I brought a few bottles in my knitting bag. Anybody want a taste?"

She filled the glasses Madame Petit-Lecourt took from a cupboard. Needles, pipes and knitting were laid down. They sipped delicately, then greedily emptied the glasses which the Widow Gros-Douillette refilled.

"If anybody in the township makes better currant wine than this I don't know about it."

"Must be because a widow's got a special touch with currants," Aristote Fait-Toute suggested.

To keep from laughing they picked up their pipes and knitting and darning.

"So then the Notary filled his pillow, he stuffed it till it was so round the seams were ready to burst and I finished sewing it up. When the Notary took his pillow away with him he said to me, he just about yelled: 'If you break your secret oath you'll be breaking the chain that keeps my ghost in my coffin.'

"I can't tell you what the Notary stuffed his burial pillow with, but if anybody here's got a pillow with that stuffing in it he could go all the way around the world!"

She picked up the bottle and refilled the glasses.

"How about your ceiling, Aristote?"

"My ceiling?" he grumbled. "It ain't my ceiling, it's the Notary's."

Silence. No one spoke. If a word came to someone's lips he drowned it in a draught of wine. The silence was a trap held out to Aristote, a trap that he'd be caught in. The glasses were empty. Aristote refilled his. The bottle was passed around. As it was drained, the wine seemed to be laughing.

"There's nothing hidden in the Notary's ceiling. There ain't no more treasure up there than there is in my pockets."

As proof he turned his pockets inside out: a few coins and shreds of tobacco fell to the floor. The others looked at him, their expressions tormenting him like an irritating summer mosquito.

"If I ain't telling the truth about that ceiling, let the bare baby Jesus break my pipe right here in my mouth."

There wasn't even a glimmer of lightning near his pipe.

Madame Petit-Lecourt disappeared into the other room; you could hear her heels on the oak floor, hear a key turning in a lock, hear the tinkling of glass. She came back with an armful of bottles borrowed from the New Notary.

"Today," she said, "is a day to be generous."

"There's no treasure hidden in the Notary's ceiling," Aristote repeated.

"If there's nothing in there how come you swore an oath to the Notary not to say what you hid inside it?"

The Seamstress asked her question with the eyes of a child pulling the wings off a fly.

"If you can't tell us about the ceiling tell us about the trip you took to Florida as soon as the plaster was dry."

"It was the first trip I ever took in my life. I didn't even take a honeymoon when I was young."

The Postman's Widow drained her glass in one aggressive gulp.

"The plaster on the ceiling was still wet and you and your wife were on the plane heading for millionaires' country, first class."

"We had to go first class. My wife was scared of that plane like it was her own coffin."

"And you stayed in a hotel where a woman has to wear a hat even if she's bare naked. I hear you even had a little palm tree growing in your room. And was there really a little stream at the foot of the bed?"

The Postman's Widow held out her glass to be refilled. The men stopped smoking, the women stuck their needles in their knitting. Aristote was about to receive the fatal blow.

"And where were you, with your pockets full of money, when your wife went to bed early because she couldn't take the sun?"

"Listen," the Carpenter protested, "it's normal for a normal man to chase women like he'd chase after a fortune."

"But when your late wife saw the lipstick marks all over your cotton summer underwear she got the idea of doing a little inspection and what did she find inside your shoes? Pictures of chippies that you paid to put lipstick wherever you wanted. That's what killed her, your poor late wife. And if it wasn't for the Notary's damn ceiling she'd still be here with us."

"Quietly drinking her little glass of wine."

"My wife was a good woman: the good Lord didn't

make them any better," said Aristote, remembering distant things in the past. "But a French Canadian's got a hard life. Like all the rest of us, my wife had more soup in her blood than iron. And then she got a germ that was bigger than her. The only thing I shouldn't'a done was to take her to Florida. The sun in the middle of the winter made that germ grow and she wasn't big enough for it. She cracked. In the end, Florida did that germ more good than my wife."

The Postman's Widow thought she'd cut the jugular vein of the animal she was hunting: Aristote Fait-Toute was a vigorous man. She drained her glass like an old soldier on his way to the front. The Postman's Widow was about to deliver another blow.

"The work I do puts blisters and calluses and scratches on my hands, but it don't make me rich. Work never makes a worker rich unless he gets the chance to hide a fortune in a ceiling. If the worker's a good boy and he hides the treasure in the ceiling where the Notary told him to, that worker won't get rich. But—I say *but*—if the worker just pretends he's hiding the treasure in the Notary's ceiling, pretends, I'm saying, and he really hides it somewhere else, well then he can go to Florida and watch his wife die while he gets tickled by all the chippies in the United States. That worker can even go on a pilgrimage to see his chippies after his wife's passed away!"

This time the animal was shaken. The Postman's Widow drank from the bottle.

"I can't defend myself," Aristote stammered, "on account of that damn oath."

Shuddering with contempt for Aristote, the Postman's Widow knocked over her glass and currant wine dripped between her fingers.

"That filthy Aristote had lipstick on him from his neck down to his belly-button, so I hear, and even lower down. Chippies' lipstick costs a fortune, so I hear. And Aristote Fait-Toute found that fortune in the Notary's ceiling."

She looked up to the ceiling, pointed her finger and shouted:

"There!"

She picked up a chair, moved it under the spot she had pointed to and climbed up on the chair. Her finger pointed to the same spot on the ceiling.

"There," she repeated.

The Shoemaker went over to Aristote and maternally filled his glass. Aristote was breathing hard, as though he'd been punched in the belly.

"A treasure in the ceiling," he said with an effort, "sometimes it's like a treasure in a pillow. It just flies away without leaving behind any feathers. The Notary was dead, we'd waked him for three days. And three nights. The whole parish and lots of foreigners besides came to see that man that was so educated he could write papers nobody but him could read. People said: 'He looks like he's asleep.' When they heard a good story they'd go outside to laugh. So they wouldn't wake him up. When it was time to close the coffin Imelda Boucher, the Seamstress . . ."

"The Notary's name was Amédée," Imelda interrupted. "I think the angels in Heaven gave me the idea. I read in my missal *Amo Deum. Amo Deum*, that means I love the Lord. *Amo Deum*, Amédée, it's practically the same thing. *Amo Deum*, Amédée, that was the nicest thing you could put on the pillow where the Notary was going to sleep till the end of time."

"When Imelda Boucher came in with her embroidered pillow the Notary's widow kissed the words *Amo Deum* but she didn't touch her Amédée. The Curé blessed him, everybody got down on their knees, the chief undertaker lifted up the dead man's head and they buried the Notary. At the funeral nobody noticed that the Seamstress was walking a little more carefully than usual. The money that was inside the Notary's pillow wasn't there any more, it was in Imelda Boucher's bloomers. The bills were tickling her bum and that's why she was walking like an altar-boy that has to go while the Curé's reading the Holy Gospel. But nobody noticed, not even the dead man!"

The bottle slipped from Imelda Boucher's hands and broke, spattering the others' legs. Madame Petit-Lecourt was already brandishing a mop.

"It was the truth that sent that bottle flying," said Aristote.

"We'll see where the truth is," Madame Petit-Lecourt shouted.

The mop stopped picking up shreds of glass and wiping up the currant wine; its handle whirled and the end was rammed into the plaster ceiling. The spear struck, frenzied, went through in several places, piercing holes. The ceiling cracked, the cracks spread, it burst and finally fell down in a cloud of clinging dust, disembowelled.

"We're going to find out the truth!"

Imelda Boucher the Seamstress grabbed a broom, the Shoemaker climbed up on the table. They ripped and tore and slashed at the ceiling. Aristote Fait-Toute was paralysed. Dust kept raining down, a gritty, suffocating cloud. All the plaster was down, the sheets of insulation torn to shreds. Hands clutched at beams and bodies swung from the ceiling; eyes peered under the edge of plaster dust. A beam cracked and gave way. They fell to the floor with a victorious cry, then climbed back to the ceiling to make another breach. The joists and floor-boards of the next storey appeared.

"We can see the truth," said Madame Petit-Lecourt. "Aristote Fait-Toute took everything."

"He didn't leave nothing for us."

Shoulders white with plaster as though he'd come through a snowstorm, pale and prostrate, Aristote left the room, showing neither anger nor remorse. The snow was white, a little hard; like plaster, it creaked beneath his feet. He thought of Florida and smiled. He could never return to that distant sunny land.

"When you look for the truth in life," said Madame Petit-Lecourt, "you're bound to get dirty."

She started cleaning up the room.

"I say we've found the real truth," said the Postman's Widow. "The Notary once wrote in a letter 'If you're as poor as poor Saint Job lift up your eyes to the sky. There you'll find a treasure.' The Notary wrote that with his own hands. And if you lift your eyes up to the sky, what do you see? The ceiling. The Notary's treasure must'a been in the ceiling if Aristote Fait-Toute put it in the ceiling."

"You trying to tell us the Notary used to write you letters?" the Shoemaker asked with a smile as pointed as a dagger.

"If you knew anything about the laws of the Post Office you'd know that any correspondence that might be dangerous has to be read, judged and communicated to the authorities and the RCMP."

"Was there a serious danger?"

"My little nose can sniff danger from far away. The Notary was on a trip. To Greece. That's in the Old Countries."

"It's real dirty in the Old Countries," Madame Petit-Lecourt told them. "Over there they'd just leave all this plaster dust on the floor and walk on it for years and centuries."

"That's the truth: how many Canadian soldiers came back from the Old Countries after the war with their secret parts all chewed up by the germs that go on eating as long as there's any meat?"

"When the Notary came back from Greece with his skin nicely cooked by the sun in that beautiful country, he used to come and mail letters to the Old Countries. I stuck on the stamps. I stayed there behind my wicket but my spit went over to the Old Countries on those stamps. All his letters were addressed to the same person. And that person used to send him letters that had pretty coloured stamps on them, like flowers. The Notary wrote more and more letters and his letters got heavier and heavier on my scales. The letters from Greece got fatter just to look at, with their bouquets of stamps. So my woman's intuition told me: 'I wonder if those are poison flowers?' I did my duty as the Postmistress and I opened a letter. I unstuck the flap of the envelope in the steam from my electric kettle. And that letter from Greece, it was written in real French and it said, I remember like it was yesterday: 'Love, don't tell me your age is an obstacle, I want to love you forever.' Where'd I put my purse?"

It was on her lap. She looked inside it, found something.

"I got something to read you."

She took out a letter and unfolded it with trembling piety. The paper was worn from being read and re-read.

"Dear Maryitsa, dear, dear, dearest Maryitsa (it's hard to read because it's the Notary's writing), Maryitsa my love, I'm copying a poem for you that a Greek wrote to the Greek girl he adored:

We must harvest while the fruit is ripe,
O my young love, my heart's delight.

The only book I care about is this book of poems. It talks about you, Maryitsa, only you. I'll burn all my other books, Maryitsa. I'm crazy, Maryitsa, my love."

"See, he said himself he was crazy!"

The Postman's Widow held the letter towards the window to have more light. She continued reading:

"I went back to our family house where an old aunt of mine is still living in her old age and I went up to the attic and got these books that I studied in my youth in my Greek courses where it was so sweet to dream. I want to read them again because they bring me closer to you. This morning, I read in one of my books that when a Greek person died they put in his grave everything he needed to continue a life on earth. Isn't it fine to live life so much? The dead person was buried with his clothes and bread and wine and weapons. Isn't it fine to refuse death like that? Maryitsa, I love you too much to die. When I die, Maryitsa, I won't really die. I'll ask them to put in my coffin everything my body needs to go on its way as far as your sunny country, and you, Maryitsa, who are more luminous than light. In life our two bodies are separate, but perhaps death will be powerful enough to reunite what was separated by life. I'll follow your ancestors' lessons and I'll prepare for my death the way you prepare for a long journey. A journey to our love, Maryitsa."

"You can guess why the Notary's coffin was opened last fall."

"The Notary must'a fought like a soul in Purgatory."

The Postman's Widow gripped the letter, holding it in the light from the window so that she could read. An invisible whip ripped the letter; the shreds dropped onto her paralysed hands.

"Could it be the passage of the dead man's soul?"

"A man's never dead . . ."

The Postman's Widow found the bottle of wine and avidly took comfort from it.

"The Notary went on writing till the very end. But that whore of a Maryitsa hadn't answered him for a long time."

She held up another letter taken from her bag.

"This is the very last letter he wrote her before the day he died." She unfolded it with infinite care. "Maryitsa darling (I think the Notary knew he was going to die because his hand was shaking when he wrote, like somebody that's scared) I remember with delight every place on your body where my lips have placed the flower of my kisses, but I don't remember if you have notaries in your country. Darling Maryitsa, how could you have offered your body to a notary one June night? Notaries aren't good looking because they wear their eyes out looking at money. They don't have nice bodies because they spend their lives bending over money and counting it; they don't know how to love because all they see is other people busy counting. Maryitsa darling, all my life I've been condemned to be what I hate most in the world: a notary, a man who doesn't speak very loud, who doesn't laugh very loud, who walks slowly so he won't be robbed of the rolls of money he's counted so fervidly. All my life I've been tied to money, like a man tied to a woman he doesn't love. I've been so unlucky in my lifetime it can't go on throughout eternity. God is fair, he'll let me find my way to you and offer you, as your ancestors did, the gifts that I'll bring with me in my coffin."

The Postman's Widow held the letter against her breast:

"For months that little whore of a Maryitsa didn't give him a sign of life and I could see the Notary wasting away. I knew Maryitsa's handwriting as well as I knew my own. I could have . . . I wrote my letter and signed it Maryitsa, but it was too late—the Notary died during the night."

She held the Notary's letter as though it were a child.

"Sleep, dear child," she said, giving the letter a little peck.

Winter went on. Like time. The snow was reflected in the light of the sky, which conferred on it an eternal tranquillity. From time to time a car would go along the grey street, with strips of ice hanging from it. Often a skidoo would rumble through the distant fields. The villagers rushed from one house to another, huddled into the wind, faces hidden in their fur collars. You saw mostly women. The men had gone off to the woods, looking for money. The days followed one another slowly; and slowly the villagers accompanied them. Sometimes when they looked up it seemed that the sun was too far away, the ground too heavy with ice and snow. And sometimes the men would try to judge how much snow the sky contained. It had been falling every winter for centuries and it would continue to fall every winter to come for still more centuries; every winter the sky shook down a sea of snow that drowned the entire earth—except for a few warm countries for the rich.

"If the good Lord really loved us he wouldn't send us snow to shovel, he'd send us gold."

And someone always replied:

"Maybe he sends us snow instead of gold because he does love us."

On the white snow of memory drifted a white Cadillac, silent as the wind. And the image of Monsieur Bourdage at the Auberge was revived. The winter winds had not chased away the words this man had sown at the Auberge; the cold had not frozen the river of dreams.

"He said if we dug the ground under our feet we'd find as much gold as there is snow."

"If it was true, we'd know."

"We've always dug just deep enough to find our pittance and bury our dead. We never dug deep enough to find our dreams."

That night a shot rang out in the silence: the dry sound of breaking ice. There was no echo. A crackling like a stone tearing through the cold. People spoke of nothing but the blood stain on the snow which they examined, blood on the ice that they could touch, that left red stains under their fingernails when it melted; they spoke of nothing but the shape of a man imprinted on the snow, of the family that lived in a frame house, up above, that had never been painted—the family of Constantin Généreux. The same words drifted through tobacco smoke everywhere in the village, the same stories circulated in the steam from kettles where meat and cabbage were boiling, the same condemnations were passed from one house to the next.

"Money that's earned dishonestly always gets its revenge in the end."

The sun glowed like a flame, but the north wind clawed at the air. Winter would reign for a long time yet. Some people came back to look at the bloodstain; they noticed that it had grown larger.

"The same thing happens with pig's blood. It's in the nature of blood to keep spreading indefinitely."

"Everybody eats pork, but Constantin Généreux, he'd be a bit tough."

"Constantin Généreux never earned an honest penny in his whole life."

"If anybody in this country ever seen Constantin Généreux do a lick of work I'd like to hear about it."

"The good Lord's fair: when he makes a man lazy he don't forget to give him the same amount of brains."

It was true that without ever exerting himself, Constantin Généreux had been able to make his family happy as those whose fathers killed themselves at work; they ate as well as families whose fathers wore themselves out working. As winter leaves wrinkles on the roads, time leaves lines on faces, but the youthful face of Constantin Généreux was intact. At night the strong winds blew in gusts that clawed at the houses, but Constantin Généreux's house didn't suffer any more than those of men exhausted by their work. From the chimney of his house on the hill you could see as much smoke as from any other chimney.

"Is it brains? Or luck?

"Lots of times wickedness seems like brains—or luck."

"Anyway, everybody dies in the end," said a man looking at his reddened fingernails.

"And when it's a rifle that puts the end to the story you know it isn't the story of the Blessed Virgin and the baby Jesus."

"I don't say it's Constantin Généreux that fired that rifle. It takes an effort to pull a trigger and Constantine's a lazy man."

During the winter when they were so far away, so alone, when just by worrying about the too rigidly white horizon you found that you liked the people you saw wrapped up in their wool and furs, laughter, echoing laughter of times past, would stir up stories of the adventurous life of Constantin Généreux. The stories spread from the amused mouths of the men who talked, and they gently spread a foliage of laughter over the tragic flower of blood frozen on the snow.

Chou Racine was telling the story. One morning, he got in his car. What was going on? The seat was lower than usual. He felt as though he were sitting on the ground. Goddamn drinking! Remorse formed a lump in his throat. He'd got drunk again the night before. One of these days alcohol would put his senses out of order: the doctor had warned him. Chou Racine started the motor, which coughed a little in the autumn air. Reverse. He let out the clutch. The car backed up with difficulty, making a noise like a locomotive that's gone off the rails. Chou Racine jumped out of the car, terrified. It had no tires. It was sitting on the rims of its wheels. Weeping with rage, fists raised towards the cross on the church, questioning the villagers one after the other and looking as though he'd made up his mind to carve them so he could read in their consciences whether they had stolen his tires. Chou Racine went to see Gros-Douillette. Gros-Douillette was still alive then, and he ran a garage.

"Taking the tires off my car, that's like stealing my feet."

"You couldn't'a picked a better time," Gros-Douillette announced after listening to Chou Racine's sad tale; "I just got four tires, practically new, and you can have them for next to nothing. Practically new."

Chou Racine bought them, paid cash. A few hours later he was at the parish limits, on a road that was more like an animal path, repairing a culvert the rain had washed away. A provincial police car approached. Chou Racine gestured to it to stop, because of the trench across the road. The car had already stopped Chou Racine saw an officer walk out of the cloud of dust he had raised, gun pointing at him. With his other hand the policeman put a jack under Chou's car.

"What's going on?"

"Shut up."

The officer removed the four tires, gun still pointing at Chou Racine, and threw them into the trunk of the provincial car.

"What's going on here?"

"Shut up."

The provincial police car took off again, flinging sand and gravel on Racine. Weeping, cursing, waving his fists to Heaven, Chou Racine returned to the village on foot.

Whenever anything was stolen in the village, or in the township, Constantin Généreux was always suspected. It was proved that he had stolen Chou Racine's tires and sold them to Gros-Douillette. Constantin Généreux swore on his children's heads that the tires had been a gift from a big-hearted widow who wanted to relieve the misery of the poor Généreux children. The charitable widow had made him swear never to whisper her name.

"Good thing," said Constantin Généreux, "there's people like that in the world to relieve the misery of the poor."

The provincial police began an investigation: all the widows in the area swore they'd never given a present to the little man who was always trying to get under their skirts. Then Constantin Généreux confessed that he'd bought the tires for a very low price from a polite young man who looked very much like the son of the local M. P.

"He's never told the truth in his life."

"That kind of life should end with a rifle shot!"

Joseph-with-the-hand-cut-off had a story to tell too. One day, in the full light of noon, there was a clamour of terrified and desperate cackling wings in his henhouse. Was it the end of the world for his hens? Joseph-with-the-hand-cut-off grabbed his rifle and ran to the henhouse, to the site of the massacre. He didn't see a wolf or a raccoon or a fox, but he did see Constantin Généreux bending over a pile of hens with trembling wings. He was selecting the plumpest ones.

"Get yourself out of my hens, by Christ!"

Constantin Généreux looked up, but he didn't seem surprised, because he continued his careful inspection of the finest hens.

"Get out of my hens or I shoot!"

Constantin Généreux looked up at Joseph-with-the-hand-cut-off.

"You hear what the Curé said in church in the middle of mass last Sunday? He said my wife's a hen, and somebody told me that in Latin 'hen' means a loose woman."

"Out of here, you son-of-a-bitch!"

"I'm too poor to have my own hen, so if I want to find out what a hen looks like, I gotta go and see somebody that does."

"You son-of-a-bitch," threatened Joseph-with-the-hand-cut-off, "I'm gonna shoot you, because I can't wring your neck with just one hand!"

"You're talking pretty hard, Joseph, to a poor man that's married to a hen."

Constantin Généreux was holding at eye level a hen that was uttering soul-rending cackles; he examined it closely, then gently put it down.

"If I see your face in my henhouse again I'm gonna crucify you!"

"It's easy to see that you're married to a woman, Joseph; me, my wife's a hen."

Constantin Généreux was about to weep. Joseph-with-the-hand-cut-off was sorry he'd yelled a little loud. Constantin Généreux left the chicken-coop looking as though he were carrying all the hunger in the world in his belly. He was bent over. Walking with difficulty. Joseph counted his hens; two were missing. Constantin Généreux had taken away in his coat the two hens whose throats he'd had time to slit.

"He's been getting ready for that gunshot for a long time."

Tristesse Lachance, like the others, was unable to feel any anger, even slight, towards Constantin Généreux: he couldn't bring himself to believe in so much wickedness. When he told about how he had been cheated by Constantin Généreux it was as though he was starting a story he didn't really believe. It happened in the winter. Tristesse Lachance saw Constantin Généreux, who had come in without knocking, walk into his kitchen. They could hear the wind roaring that day, but there was a good fire singing in the wood stove. Constantin's hands were red, scratched by the claws of the cold and his too large overcoat with the buttons done up wrong was covered with patches of snow, as though he'd fallen down several times. He asked, barely loud enough to be heard:

"Will you give me a hand? I can't do anything."

Tristesse Lachance led him over to the stove. While he held his hand feebly over the fire, Tristesse poured him a brandy with a few drops of milk. Gradually the snow melted on his shoulders, his hands forgot the claws of the cold and he regained the power of speech. Constantin Généreux needed the help of some charitable soul. His children were crying in the house, his wife had kicked him out into the storm after humiliating him with every insult, even wishing for his death; his wife had never understood how sick he was, an invalid almost. The doctor had shown him a photograph of his heart: it looked like a potato eaten by insects. He had the heart, the kidneys and the lungs of a man of ninety, "ninety years worn-out," but his wife didn't believe him. She mistreated him. His last log was burning in the stove; when it was gone there'd be nothing but embers left to heat the house; after that, there'd be only hot ashes, then cold ones. The children were crying, his wife had sent him outside to die. Constantin was so sick. How could he go and cut wood? All he could expect from his heart now was feeble beating that kept a man alive but prevented him from living like a man. All effort was forbidden. Working would mean crushing his heart the way you crush a wild strawberry when you step on it. Oh, he didn't want charity! But how could he cut his wood?

"Have you got any wood at least?" Tristesse Lachance inquired.

"A few logs, but what I haven't got is the strength to saw them up. But since I gotta make a choice between dying and my children freezing, I'm gonna cut them some wood so my poor children can live till spring. I was lucky some charitable soul gave me the wood. I'll thank that person till the end of my days. I wish I could live longer so I could go on thanking that person. I got the wood but I ain't got the health or the strength."

The soul of Tristesse Lachance was drowned in goodness. He wanted to contain the wave but he couldn't. He dressed himself in sweaters, a red checkered shirt, his leather cap with fur ear-flaps, and picked up his electric chain-saw. There was a stack of old fence wood behind Constantin Généreux's house: a few pickets and a few posts. The chain-saw cut into the wood, dried by so many summers, with grating pleasure. It was cedar, and the fire would attack with a hearty appetite. It was such an easy job that Tristesse Lachance decided to cut the whole pile of fence wood. He'd have liked to buy the wood to use on his land but he thought that Constantin Généreux needed wood more than money. He cut. Cut. With the joy of one who is being useful to another man. Christian joy. The Généreux family would have fire for the winter. Constantin couldn't find words to express his gratitude. He promised that if God miraculously restored his sick heart and blood he'd work a whole summer—without pay—for Tristesse Lachance, who picked up his chain saw and went home, his soul content. Winter dragged on. From time to time Tristesse Lachance would stop to contemplate the white smoke coming out of the Généreux chimney; he felt good then, and his pride was as great as his goodness. The fire heating that poor house came from his own good heart. Slowly winter disappeared, like a bird flying higher and higher in the sky. Then it was spring. When the earth was dry at the beginning of summer, Tristesse Lachance, as his father before him and he himself had done for years, walked his land from top to bottom, right to the end. But where was the end? He recognized the black spruce trees, the stones, the knolls and bushes, but he couldn't find the limit of his land: the fence had disappeared.

"A fence don't jump the fence like a horse. Where's my fence?"

He suddenly remembered the soft white smoke from the Généreux chimney, the dry cedar, the fence wood he had sawed up with such goodness to warm the winter for the Généreux family.

"From a thief to a gunshot, it's the same road, as the poet says," one of the men remarked.

"What poet?"

Fred Bouffard had seen all the houses in the country; he'd set foot, both feet and all the rest, in all the houses in the country to sell insurance policies that would make rich all the widows and anyone who had the misfortune to cut off an arm or a leg. One day Fred Bouffard said to Constantin Généreux:

"Constantin, you got a wife and kids and a little house; and you got the right to a future too. A future after you die. A future that'll give something to your wife and kids, who haven't got the right to a future because their father hasn't got one. You can't go without giving them a future. And I can sell you one. There's thousands of dollars waiting in the banks."

"Waiting for me to die."

"How would you feel if nobody was around to look after your wife and kids that you haven't provided for after you die? Do you want your wife and kids to starve to death after you die because their father hasn't bought them a future?"

"I'll buy your future off you if the price is right. Come over to the house tonight."

Fred Bouffard went. Madame Constantin Généreux was waiting behind the screen door, which she opened for him. He went in. Holding the door open with her outstretched arm, she blocked the doorway so he couldn't avoid grazing her bosom with his shoulder. He could feel it burning.

"Your old man around?"

She adjusted the tucks on the cotton blouse that was stretched by her large breasts.

"He's gonna be late again. That's the only thing he knows how to do, come in late. And I'm a woman that waits. Oh! there's a spot on my blouse !"

She scratched the cloth over her breast with her fingernail; Fred imagined it as hard as wood.

"I'm all dirty! We may be poor but we want to be clean like everybody else."

Suddenly she unbuttoned her blouse, and her breasts popped out. Fred Bouffard's legs disappeared.

"I better be going."

Before he'd taken a step, two arms crushed him against

a burning, panting body. Fred Bouffard fell into a dizzying flame. Was it Hell? Was it Heaven? He wanted to repeat "I better be going," but he'd lost his voice. Madame Constantin Généreux let herself fall against him. He collapsed onto her. Suddenly something cold struck him on the chin. He opened his eyes. The black barrel of a rifle. Constantin Généreux was ready to press the trigger. He threatened:

"I'm in a state of legitimate defense! The law says I can kill you. Fred Bouffard, you're trying to take my wife, the only treasure the good Lord's seen fit to give me. Damn you, Bouffard! You're trying to steal my wife and I'm gonna kill you!"

Madame Constantin Généreux pulled herself out from under Fred Bouffard, who was paralyzed and trembling.

"It's a matter of honour. Poor people have their honour too! That's all we got. You can try and steal my woman but you won't steal my honour! You think a poor man like me's gonna walk through the village with his head up after you've humiliated my wife?"

Fred Bouffard tried to protest; when he'd whispered the first syllable the barrel of the rifle nailed his head to the floor.

"Fred Bouffard, you ain't gonna walk through the village with your head up neither after you've made erotic contact with Madame Constantin Généreux in spite of her consent and trying to perpetuate a rape."

Constantin Généreux used the vocabulary of his beloved *Allô Police*, in which every Sunday he read religiously the lyrical accounts of the crimes of the week.

"Fred Bouffard, I'm going to pound your head down to your feet!"

The barrel of the rifle pressed a little harder on Fred Bouffard's chin.

"I'm gonna talk about this rape right across the country; that'll help your business. Husbands are gonna trust you!"

"I'll pay. What's your price?"

"There's no price for the rape of the wife of a poor sick man. It'll cost you a lot! You're gonna pay through the nose, my friend!"

Fred paid through the nose.

"Money's always got a curse on it," said one of the smokers.

"Every cent Constantin Généreux earned had a bigger curse on it than the one before!"

Several times, Constantin Généreux hid with his rifle behind the small curtain that closed off the door to a bedroom on the ground floor; several times his wife suddenly uncovered her bosom, throwing herself at the neck of a man who had come to bring a letter or parcel or to sell something. Several times he sold his silence to these men who feared scandal and their own wives.

Constantin, who had used his wife as bait, decided to use his daughters when they had stopped being children. The girls seemed to have been made by a loving angel and a passionate she-devil: their eyes were filled with grace and sin. One night Constantin Généreux found himself alone with his three daughters. The mother had signed a contract with the Government: she was going to teach catechism and geography to little Indians in the Gaspé. They knew in the village that Madame Constantin Généreux could read a little, but not catechism! They were amazed, then, that the Government had picked her to teach catechism and geography to the little Indians in the Gaspé. "Good thing they're Indians!" No one in the village knew, of course, that an official from the Department of Colonization had tried to rape Madame Généreux. Luckily Constantin had arrived in time to save his wife's honour. The official had agreed to pay for his sin, and Madame Généreux went to teach Catholic civilization to the little Indians in Gaspé.

"Girls," said Constantin Généreux, "we're all alone. This is the first time in your life you've had to get along without your mother. We'll be all alone for a few months. I don't like it too much for pretty girls like you to be without their mother, because a pretty girl needs her mother till she makes her own pretty girl. Your mother's gone off to the Indians in the Gaspé because your mother's a saint. You've been to school and I hope you learned that a saint's always got some suffering, some wound. Your blessed mother's wound is me: always weak, always sick, can't work, can't even bend my back to pick up a hunk of gold if there was one in front of me. I'd'a liked to bring you up like princesses, but I'm a sick man, a weak man, a man that got old before his time; like the doctor said, I'm just a breath between youth and old age. Your blessed mother's gone far away so we can have bread on our table this winter. It's the good Lord's will that I'm a sick man and I accept his curse. So I'm sick. But not blind! I got good eyes and I've seen with my own eyes that the boys come to the house and prowl and sniff and nose around like bees around the flowers. I even seen with my own good eyes when the boys come up in their cars or on their motorcycles that you get even prettier, like flowers. That's normal, it's natural, it's the way the good Lord made life. You're pretty girls, and beautiful flowers like you are a gift from the good Lord. I think I had to sacrifice my health to earn all this beauty around my table. God must'a said up there in Heaven: 'Constantin, do you want to be a father as strong as a maple tree with daughters as ugly as lice, or do you want to be a puny, sickly, skinny father with daughters as beautiful as the day?' And I must'a told the good Lord, down here on earth in my little frame house, I must'a said: 'God, give me daughters as beautiful as the day; they'll be wealth and consolation to a poor, suffering, useless man.' If you got a fortune like that you don't want to lose it. You girls are young and you don't know the dangers in life. I want to watch over your education and I'm going to ask you not to go running off into the woods. You're pretty flowers and you're gonna stay where you grew. The bees can come to you and you can wait for them."

The three girls listened without touching their crusts of bread, without drinking their glasses of milk, without picking at their plates: a few clouts in their childhood had taught them it was better to listen to their father's quavering voice.

"It's true our house is pretty small. God didn't make me strong enough to get rich and buy us a big one. Sometimes a boy and a girl want to whisper in each other's ears. This is a small house, but my girls have got as much right as anybody else to have sweet nothings whispered in their ears. Even more, because they're more beautiful. You got two bedrooms already and I've decided to give you mine. Three rooms, one for each of you. I'll sleep under the kitchen table. No, don't say no! I'll do it because I love you. The boys are gonna come and when you want them to tickle your ears with love words you can go in your rooms. That way you'll all be here with me and I can keep an eye on my flowers and the bees that come to gather honey. I can keep an eye on your education."

At night the boys came as usual, spinning on motorcycles, racing their motors, raising dust; some slowed down when they passed the frame house, others speeded up, and they all shouted words that made the Généreux girls blush as they sat on the swing like well brought-up young ladies in their brightly coloured dresses. They answered by laughing or waving their hands. As a matter of fact, the boys were rather afraid of the nasty little man who was the father of these pretty girls. His tricks and the damage he'd done had been described so often–but the girls' beauty, their laughter and their rounded breasts erased their father's sins. The girls got off the swing and leaned on the fence beside the road. The boys stopped. They talked. They laughed. When the night was dark, the girls invited them in. They were surprised to find the little house, so sad on the outside, clean and even gay within. Constantin Généreux had gone out. The boys no longer laughed coarsely: they made sounds that wafted through the air like the mooing of contented oxen. Now they talked with a certain gentleness, a certain music in their voices. Soon they wanted to whisper secrets. And the girls held out their little ears, hidden by their curls. The boys' beards caught in their hair. Sometimes their whispers evoked hearty laughs. Then the boys didn't laugh. The youngest girl said:

"We could talk easier up in my room."

The boys left the girls' rooms very late. The sun was up before the last one left.

Constantin waited in the kitchen, sitting at the table. Silently he held out his hand. The girls didn't understand. He remained silent, hand extended. They looked at one another and didn't understand.

"What do you want?" asked the youngest.

His answer was his outstretched hand. The girls didn't dare to speak or move. Suddenly all the anger in the world exploded in his mouth.

"The money!" he roared.

The girls looked at one another, not understanding.

"What money?"

Constantin Généreux kept his hand out; he spoke without shouting this time, in his usual small voice.

"What? Those boys spent the night in your rooms and they didn't have enough honour to pay for their board?"

He dropped his hand. His voice was wrapped in tenderness.

"Those boys owe you something."

His voice was filled with goodness. The girls loved their father.

"You're worth more than those boys think."

The boys returned. Next morning, Constantin Généreux, sitting at the kitchen table, held out his hand again. The girls were proud to put some bills in his hand. He divided them into three piles on the tablecloth.

"I'll take my share because I'm your father. And I'll take a share for your blessed mother; you owe her something because she made you the way you are, pretty and well brought up. Some day she'll be old and she won't be able to go to the Gaspé to earn her bread among the Indians, and the man she's married to's a sick man that can't give her the kind of life she deserves. The third share's for the three of you. I'll put it in the bank and when you want to get married I'll give you your dowries like a respectable father."

The boys didn't wait until night to come back. There were cars and motorcycles parked in front of the sad little house in the afternoon. The boys brought their friends and soon the girls didn't leave their rooms at all. Constantin Généreux himself stood at the door of his house and saw to it that everything proceeded properly.

Sometimes his wife would write from the Gaspé and he would dictate his reply to the youngest daughter, the one with the nicest handwriting:

"My dearest wife, we have the best girls in the world and those children are going to help us have a fine happy old age . . ."

One morning in November Constantin Généreux said:

"Girls, you're young, you have to enjoy the beautiful things God created. Enjoy them while you're young. When you aren't young any more you get like me: sick and sad and weak. The summer sun in the middle of the winter must be one of the most beautiful things that God created. I'll send you to Florida after Christmas if you want. All I ask is a little help."

That very day Constantin Généreux noticed an increased revenue. His best transaction was without a doubt the one he concluded with Auguste Albert.

"How much would it cost me to spend the whole afternoon and the whole evening and the whole night in the room?"

"Who with?"

"The oldest."

"This is the first time. Nobody ever asked me for that before."

Auguste Albert's face shone with delight. "The first time!"

His beaming did not escape Constantin Généreux.

"It'll be an honour for my oldest girl. How much do you make a week? I hope it's more than a poor sick father that can't work."

Auguste Albert opened his billfold, took out a cheque and tossed it on the tablecloth. Constantin read the figures printed on it.

"Sign it; I'll take it. Don't forget—my daughter's doing you a favour and an honour."

Auguste Albert spent the afternoon in the oldest girl's bedroom, and the evening and the night. Before Constantin woke up he left, taking with him the oldest girl. At dawn, they knocked at the Curé's door, who heard their confession and agreed to marry them to avoid the mortal sin of living together without his benediction. In the first light of morning Auguste Albert raced the motor of his dented convertible and it sprang forward like a crazed horse. When they came back from their honeymoon they moved into the house of Auguste Albert's mother, a lonely old lady who told the young bride:

"If my boy'd asked my advice I'd'a told him to look somewhere else for a wife. I wouldn't want my grandchildren to have Constantin Généreux's poisoned blood in their veins. But my boy married you and I'll give you all the room. Just leave me enough for my last breath. I'll give you my place, you pretty child, but don't try to bury me right away."

Before supper, night had replaced the day. Auguste Albert ate his soup. It was the first soup his wife had made, from vegetables put up by Auguste's mother. The door opened, although no one had knocked.

"Hello there, children! It's me, your father, Constantin Généreux!"

Auguste went on slurping his soup. His wife was busy with her pots on the stove, and she turned her back to her father.

"Sit down and have a smoke, father-in-law," Auguste offered when he had finished his soup.

Constantin Généreux stood at the door, which he didn't close; he had dared to come inside, but he didn't dare move any farther.

"Daughter, when your old mother-in-law starts dying in your arms and when that husband of yours starts filling you with babies, I want you to know you can come back home. The door'll be open, just as if nothing happened. But you should know that the good Lord'll punish you for deserting your father that's got the bad luck to be weak and poor."

He left without closing the door. The cold air steamed in the kitchen. Auguste's wife thought that once again winter would be inevitable.

The boys kept coming to Constantin Généreux's house, but the oldest girl's empty room made him sad. All the members of a family should cooperate with one another; if one refused to help, the whole family is punished.

December: shoulders white with the first snow, Constantin arrived at Auguste Albert's. This time, his son-in-law stopped slurping his soup and didn't invite him in for a smoke.

"Daughter, you sisters are going to the sun in Florida after Christmas. While you watch the earth turn to ice, your sisters will be seeing summer. There's still room for you on the trip."

And Constantin slipped into the night like the wind. Auguste's wife closed the door.

"If I can't go to Florida with my sisters, maybe I can go with my husband."

"Me!" Auguste exclaimed. "I got my car to pay off and I gotta paint it and the muffler's shot and I gotta buy tires and get a new windshield. After I done all that, the car'll be ready but I won't be able to go to Florida because there won't be any money left."

During Christmas week Auguste decided to buy snow tires. When he came home from the garage his wife wasn't in the house. His old mother had seen her getting ready to go out, but she didn't dare ask where she was going. The old woman was making supper because the daughter-in-law hadn't come back. The son ate without speaking. He got up from the table without drinking his tea.

"I know where she is."

The snow was already deep; it had been smoothed by the wind. Auguste could feel it under his feet, as harsh as the ground. The air pinched his nostrils and it seemed to him that his lips were thicker in the cold. It would be a cold night: one of the coldest of the year. Usually there wasn't a frost like that till February. Up on the hill, a yellow light shone from the windows of Constantin Généreux's house. Auguste walked faster. He resisted knocking at the door, kicking it open instead. On the doorstep, he resisted going inside. He heard his lips, thickened by the cold, cry:

"I want my wife!"

"Come and get her!"

"Give me back your daughter; she's my wife!"

"Come and get her!"

"Wife," Auguste Albert roared, "if you love me, come here! Do you love me?"

For a reply there was a sort of distant rumbling, like a thunderbolt in Florida that he could hear in the cold snow of winter.

Constantin Généreux fired the shot that blew off his son-in-law's face.

"Some lives," said one of the smokers, "spend years and years getting ready for real bad luck."

"Some people, all they got's their bad luck."

In mid-winter, talk sustained the warmth of life. The breath of speech tried to chase away the breath of the wind. If people were silent, they might notice those old ships which haunted the depths of memory gliding to the horizon on the swell of the snow; the north wind might stir up in their souls the memories that awaken death. They spoke so as not to be heard. They spoke to drive away the silence clutching their throats. In this black jungle with its tangled silences, its cutting lianas hidden in the light, man was a sad wild creature who can only talk. When car tires squealed across the icy roads, when the motor of a snowmobile throbbed in a snowbank, it was man who roared in the great disorder, frozen and white. Winter is a long night that neglects to grow dark. Pretending to forget that it is night, men, moving like sleepwalkers, give themselves up to their habitual tasks. In the great silence, one event can stir up the blood, frozen like the sap in the trees. For more than two days, people forget that November is so far behind, that all they want now is April. Men neglect their work and get together in the kitchen with their wives. With the same gestures and the same laughter, they take up the same old story: it's as though describing the facts transforms them until they resemble what people want them to resemble.

"Japanese dingdongs! Japanese dingdongs!"

"They say they're Japanese, but . . ."

March. On the roofs, the roads, on the shoulders of the black spruce trees, there is still nothing but snow. The Japanese dingdongs arrived—it must be said—like birds in the spring! First, one dingdong: they didn't know yet that it was Japanese. It was the first one: they examined it, were amazed. Later, another: they looked at it; it reminded them of the first one. At the third, no more hesitation: they could tell there would be many. And so they were, those Japanese dingdongs!

"A man with nothing to do, that don't like rocks, can imagine there's gold nuggets in our land, and then invent dingdongs!"

"Japanese dingdongs!"

The first Japanese dingdong showed up in the church, that is, in the Auberge du Bon Boire where religious celebrations had been held since the church burned down. The electric organ, which the night before had embroidered veils of music over the body of a dancer plucking off her clothes, attempted to accompany with pious harmonies the flight of angels around the altar of God. The Curé explained that once more, God was going to die. The organ tried to sound sad and the organist dreamed that this night too the dancer would take off her clothes so he could cast veils of inspired arpeggios over her. Miss Catechism was in ecstasy. Suddenly, she fainted: she had spotted the first Japanese dingdong! The sound of her inert and pious young woman's body tumbling onto the prie-Dieu resounded up to Heaven. The Curé choked on his Latin phrase. A few parishioners were already quarrelling over Miss Catechism's outstretched body. Who would take the arms? Which arm? Who would look after the legs? Which leg? Miss Catechism, who was responsible for revealing to the children of the village the mysteries of life and religion, was taken outside the Auberge. The pages in the Curé's hands were as heavy as granite. No one was allowed to put his hands on Miss Catechism. Outside, the wind lifted her skirt and revealed to her kindly bearers some of the secrets her more quick-witted students dreamed about. The icy wind on her body opened her eyes. Speaking in a roundabout manner as though trying to walk around the moon, with motions that seemed to be trying to chase away the mosquitoes of summers yet to come, she described the last image she had seen before she fainted.

She was coming back from the Lord's Table where she had received the bread of God from the Curé's own hands—his holy hands, as beautiful as those on statues, his soft beautiful hands accustomed to holy books and prayer: "A caress is also a prayer," he had told Miss Catechism one day, "but this truth is not one to be spread around, because not everyone is enlightened enough to understand it." He had also said: "You are the child of God, with hands so pious they turn everything they touch to prayers." So Miss Catechism was coming back from the Lord's Table, a fragment of the body of God in her mouth, her eyes closed. When she felt God's warm presence in her stomach, alive, like a small child, she opened her eyes and saw—and she fell into a precipice.

The bellies of the four men who were carrying her gurgled with suppressed laughter, but their faces were imperturbable as mortuary masks. Miss Catechism selected her words, rejecting those that were vulgar, those that would provoke lewd smiles in the eyes of these honest Christian brothers; she rejected the technical, scholarly words they wouldn't understand.

"What I saw was a member. A male organ. A virile member. A male organ that was not, however, of a normal size, excuse me, I mean usual, excuse me, I mean smaller than the ones that are described in the sexual education books, because I've never seen one. I'm not married."

"Ask Monseiur le Curé. He ain't got one himself but he could ask one of his faithful parishioners to devote himself to the cause . . ."

"To make the sacrifice . . ."

The four Christians discreetly nudged one another with their elbows.

"I saw a dingdong no bigger than my little finger."

She held up her little finger—so fine, unwrinkled, carved from ivory, with a long pointed fingernail like the ones the men had seen on the beautiful girls in the magazines they hid in their cars.

"A small virile member that could belong to a child, but I've never seen a child's dingdong—I'm not a mother and there were twelve girls in our family—but it must have been a child's dingdong with its little red tip; it looked like a baby bird without feathers, all naked and weak and cold, looking for its nest. I was frightened and I fainted."

"Poor Miss Catechism," said one of the men, "if you're that scared of a little bird that hasn't got its feathers we wouldn't dare let you see a big one that has!"

To escape from the wind and her bearers, Miss Catechism went back inside the Auberge—the church—and knelt down. She looked up to the Curé at the altar. The incense, the prayers and the Latin gave him a smile that resembled the smile of God. Perhaps it was God himself whom she loved so much. The Curé had someone bring the blessed key to open the little door of the tabernacle. Following the motions prescribed in the liturgy, he held his breath; he bent over to graze the sacred stone in front of the tabernacle. But a violent flash froze him in this posture: inside the tabernacle, on the holy lace cushion, instead of God's host was a Japanese dingdong. Japanese? He didn't know yet. It looked like a slug, a bean-pod, a minnow, a small carrot, a malicious mouse. There was a child's penis in a forbidden place. His heart stopped. For a few seconds he swayed in eternity.

That Sunday, Imelda Boucher the Seamstress found a Japanese dingdong floating in her cup of tea. A woman taking a nap found one in her bed. Another put her hand in her coat pocket and touched an object—a candy or a stone. It was hard. She picked it up to look at it: she was so surprised that the Janapese dingdong leaped like a frightened grasshopper. That night Japanese dingdongs were found in a folded newspaper, in a drawer filled with fine lingerie, in a hat and in a bottle of pills. On the days that followed they were found everywhere: hanging from purse-strings and schoolboys' satchels, from women's purses and attached to coat buttons and to Madame Petit-Lecourt's chain. When Madame Chou Racine got on the bus to Quebec City there was a bouquet of Japanese dingdongs on the handle of her suitcase. The Japanese dingdongs proliferated and spread like ants. They were called Japanese because of their waxy yellow colour. There were so many that people tired of laughing at them. The first days were like a fever: they bought and sold and bought back and sold again, laughing and shaking. Complicated strategies were discussed for concealing them. Business flourished, among the hollering of surprised women and the curses of insulted males.

"Them Japanese dingdongs are an epidemic! They're like poor people's cockroaches! "

Much attention was paid to the ones Mimi Gros-Douillette wore as earrings when she went dancing at the Auberge. She was a university student. Drinking her beer from the bottle she said:

"*Calvaire*, we got to demystify sex! "

Or:

"Money's the root of the class struggle and the class struggle's going to desexualize money, *Calvaire*! "

Lumberjacks home from the woods for the weekend looked at her with pleasure, but didn't dare to listen to what she said.

"That little fucker sure sings up a storm, *Vierge*!"

In the woods they'd never seen dingdongs dangling from the ears of a fat, educated girl. They'd never seen a Japanese dingdong. Early in the evening they timidly asked the Waitress for information: what's that pretty girl wearing in her ears? Japanese, how come they're Japanese? Why's she wearing them? Where'd she get them? Where can you buy them? How much? Late in the evening, the lumberjacks had no more room for beer on their tables, which were covered with a pile of Japanese dingdongs as high as that. Never in their lives, in fact, had they drunk so little. All their attention was concentrated on business, that is on buying all the Japanese dingdongs they could find in the Auberge and in the village. They had the monopoly. Where Japanese dingdongs were concerned, they were stronger than any multinational corporation. They controlled a pile of Japanese dingdongs heaped up on their table so high they couldn't see the other side. They were the dingdong bankers, the dingdong kings: they had all the dingdongs—except for the two dangling from Mimi Gros-Douillette's ears. She had rejected all offers to buy.

"*Hostie*," she said in her language with its smattering of Latin, poetry and chemical formulae, "let the rest of the whores in this dump let go of their dingdongs, sex ain't gonna be any kind of a mystery for me."

"If you let me have two Japanese dingdongs I'll let you

have two French-Canadian ones!"

"I'll give you mine as a bonus!"

"Ha ha ha!"

To show the dingdong magnates the respect they deserved, the Aubergiste focused the yellow beam of a spotlight on the lumberjacks' table. Under the blazing sun the mountain of dingdongs glowed red. The lumberjacks, like mad kings, wanted to lay waste their kingdom. And so the dingdongs began to fall onto kissing couples, their shadows barely moving on the dance floor. At first it was a light hail: the shadows moved closer together. Then the hail became heavier and the shadows blended into one another. Suddenly the sky burst: an avalanche! The dancing shadows scurried away under the fusillade. Dingdongs rained down on all sides, striking, slapping: it was a bombardment. The customers took refuge under tables. That wasn't enough—the dingdongs lashed and flogged. Tables were overturned. Palisades were improvised from piled-up chairs. The Japanese dingdongs were shells that whistled and burst. The entrenched couples yelled with fear and delight.

Suddenly they were thirsty. The storm of Japanese dingdongs abated. Prudently, the combatants rose from behind the barricades. They disentangled chairs, legs, tables. The two Japanese dingdongs were no longer dangling from Mimi Gros-Douillette's ears.

When dawn appeared through the frost on the windows they were still drinking and still thirsty. The Aubergiste, regretfully but very politely, sent his clients, one after the other, out into the storm. Then he cleaned up the Auberge, for in a few hours the Curé would be coming to celebrate mass.

"We never come in for a drink when he's saying mass; how come he gets to say mass while we're drinking?"

"The church burned down."

"So the good Lord don't want no more mass. If the Curé keeps saying mass at the Auberge the good Lord's gonna burn it down too."

"The Curé'll build a new one when we get the money."

"He don't get one goddamn cent from me. I'll give him rocks—my land's full of them."

"You're right: gold and silver melt away but rocks last forever!"

"*Calvaire!*" Mimi Gros-Douillette interrupted; "the

Catholic church is a capitalist bank managed by men that like gold better than women."

Respectfully urged on by the Aubergiste, the drinkers left. The great icy sail of the morning snapped in the wind, which plucked the words from their lips and carried them away.

The Aubergiste pushed back the tables and distributed prie-Dieux. He transformed the bar into an altar, hung crucifixes on the walls. Then he opened several windows wide to let the winter wind—pure as the breath of God—drive away the smells of dancing and alcohol, drive away the odour of smoke and bodies entwined in the shadows, and disperse the profane butterflies of dance music. Slowly the perfume of the blue sky, white clouds and snow descended on the Auberge du Bon Boire.

The Curé entered, chalice in hand, his stride more hasty than religious. The parishioners noticed his unaccustomed speed. Rather than going to the altar, he advanced towards the faithful. Neglecting to mutter a Latin phrase, according to the ritual, he announced:

"My brothers, a great tribulation has struck our village. For a week now this tribulation has been eating at our village. For a week, my brothers, you have been watching it and roaring with laughter at it, this catastrophe that's creeping towards you with poisonous eyes. In the Olden Days, God decided to punish a people who had offended him. He unleashed the fires of Heaven on their heads and on their towns and villages. Recently, God sent fire to our village too. God destroyed our church. Another time, in the Olden Days, God sent to a people of sinners a rain of grasshoppers, a flood of grasshoppers that devoured their crops. My brothers, it's winter here in our Canada. God can't send us a flood of grasshoppers: they'd catch cold, get the flu and a cough and they wouldn't be able to destroy our crops by devouring them. So, to test us, to warn us that the time has come to repent for our sins, both present and past, God has unleashed among us a cloud, not of grasshoppers, but a cloud of . . . I don't dare to name them in this sacred and holy place because the sound alone would pain the ear of God and offend him: a cloud of small inert objects that might allegorically and metaphorically resemble grasshoppers, but which in fact evoke a part of the body that the Church advises us to keep hidden both summer and winter. This cloud has come from a distant land, foreign and pagan; this cloud has come to burden with its vice-steeped presence the nights and days of our faithful Christians, their dreams and their daydreams. My brothers, these perverse little objects also resemble rockets. They will transport your souls to those dark and viscous marshes where impure thoughts and perverse inclinations come from. Christians, bow your heads and repent. This very day, after mass, altar-boys in black soutanes, the colour of your souls, and white surplices, the colour of the pure soul, will call at each of your houses; they will hold out big bags and into them, holding your noses, I want you to throw the perverse little objects I've been talking about; dispose of them in that bag just like you'd get rid of a germ that carries the seed of death in its mandibles."

After mass one of the altar-boys fell to the Curé's feet. He wouldn't get up. He wouldn't speak. He would only sob, his forehead bathed in tears. The Curé questioned him. Asked for a cold cloth. The Aubergiste suggested giving him some cognac. The Curé offered him one of the candies he always carried in his pockets for the children. The child wept. Beneath the soutane and surplice, his body was consumed by sobs. Could his soul be sick?

"My child," said the Curé, "confess your sins. That will calm your soul."

Through his hiccups and tears the altar-boy managed to pronounce a few tear-soaked words; his fresh conscience was laboriously unveiled, one word at a time, terrified, one sigh at a time, silently. The Curé learned that the dingdongs were not Japanese.

In September a teacher had come and offered his services to the village school board. At his first meeting with the members of the board he seemed timid. He scarcely spoke, but when he opened his suitcase they saw that it was overflowing with documents. Silently, he presented his diplomas: psychology, geography, art, Latin, andragogy, geography, history: a dozen diplomas in elegant Latin or English calligraphy. A man doesn't need to speak, they concluded, when he's acquired so many diplomas.

"A man that don't talk much," said one of the members of the board, "won't have much to say before he takes the money we're offering."

"How come you're coming to our village with all those diplomas? A good pair of mitts comes in handier than a diploma up here on the mountain in the wind."

"I like the pure air. I like the peace. Up here you have Heaven for a neighbour."

"The land's full of rocks; the people aren't rich."

"The people here live in the midst of treasures, but they don't know it."

The learned man was appointed Teacher at the New School. He was never late; he was never sick. He started his lessons as soon as the electric buzzer stopped throbbing. He addressed his pupils formally, calling them "vous." He stayed late in his classroom at night to correct their work with his red pencil. They discovered that when he walked, his feet seemed to be pushing away the cumbersome skirt of a soutane. His silence was likely a kind of religious meditation that cleanses a man of earthly speech.

The Teacher was also an artist. In his institution he had been given the assignment, during his free time and holidays, of making saints. The job consisted of filling rubber moulds with liquid plaster. Then with great delicacy he would place the moulds on shelves to let the plaster dry. Several hours after he "lifted" them (to use the craftsman's terminology), then gently sanded away small rough spots on the figurines, blew away the dust and painted the clothing. An older brother would paint the eyes, the faces and the hands.

One afternoon the teacher announced to his pupils after their mathematics lesson:

"Class is over. You may leave. But if you wish to stay here I'll talk to you about art."

It was a word the pupils had never heard. And what is better than an unknown word to keep someone in his seat?

"Art is a means of crossing a frontier to go deeper into the self."

The pupils didn't understand.

"There's more to life than money; above all, there is art. Art is defined by the soul's awareness of the body."

The pupils looked at one another. One, the tallest, raised his hand.

"Monsieur, is school out?"

"Yes, Monsieur, class is over."

Jumping over desks, walking on the seats, the pupils quickly formed a jousting group at the door, a tangled, woolly, booted group.

"Those who think that life consists of squabbling on the

skating rink may leave. To the others, I would like to speak about art, which reveals unknown domains that can't be bought with gold."

The teacher walked through the impatient group of pupils at the door and unlocked it. The tallest ones, the most muscular, the ones with the biggest boots, the loudest voices, the biggest hands, fled, yelling:

"Fire!"

There remained the young, the pale, the puny, the fair ones. The teacher asked them to approach him. With the emotional voice of one who is passing on a secret laden with life and death, he told them of the existence of a land that is hidden behind appearances. He confided to them that a few privileged persons could pass behind the door into the privileged realm of art. In order to enter that kingdom they first had to be in a state of grace. Whispering, he explained.

"Now you are occupying the space of your body. Let your thoughts spread through your body, filling it as wine fills a jug, as the water fills a river. Your hands are not foreign to you now, they are your body. Think of your feet: they are not foreign, they are your body. Think of your chest, your neck. Your body is the instrument that allows you to intercept the waves of the universe. Through these waves the universe enters your body, the world vibrates in your body. Art is the way of feeling and loving and interpreting the heartbeats of the universe."

Eyes closed, the short, the thin, the puny, the coughers, the fair ones were nearly asleep, nearly dreaming, drifting through the lands of their bodies; and the Teacher's voice tickled their souls, which had grown very big inside their bodies, which they felt to be as vast as the universe.

"You must love your body: love your back, your chest, your arms, your feet; you must love your neck, your legs, your thighs; you must love . . . your penis, the little thing that hangs between your legs, the little fruit hanging from the branch of your body."

A few minutes later—because they couldn't not love their bodies, luminous and vibrating with the marvellous waves of the universe—the children had unzipped their trousers and offered to Art their scrawny little fair penises, so they could intercept the messages of the universe.

"Are you ashamed of your bodies, God's work of art?"

The children responded as in prayer:

"No!"

The children stood and squeezed their eyes shut. The waves of the universe were crackling through their bodies, with electric currents powerful enough to light up the entire village. With his tapered little nun's fingers and the pious gestures learned from his statues, the Teacher moulded in soft brown clay each little penis, which seemed to him, inside their trousers, to resemble fledglings perched in their cages; on their beaks he placed a tender kiss.

"Art is the love of the universe. Those who love only money don't understand, because they can love only money. You must learn to touch this part of your body with as much respect as your forehead, where ideas are born. God himself created it from clay. I will distribute a few coins to each of you. But first you all must swear, before God, on your own heads, to reveal nothing of what has happened here."

At school the next day the hockey players noticed that the small ones, the coughers, the skinny, the puny and the fair ones were pale, with shadows under their booodshot eyes. Their secret was so burdensome it had exhausted them. When the bell rang at the end of the day the Teacher said:

"Those who love Art are to stay with me."

They didn't dare to look at one another or to hesitate. They formed a circle "imitating the perfection of the universe," and then the Teacher ordered them to close their eyes and hold our their hands. In them he gently placed the small shapes he had moulded in plastic and painted with the brush that had been used to paint the mouths and eyes of saints.

"Do you love the part of your body that contains your entire body? as your bodies contain the entire universe? Do you love it?"

And the small children's voices responded, as in a prayer at church:

"Yes!"

"Children, you must proclaim it publicly, to the four corners of your village!"

The small ones, the puny, the skinny, the coughers and the fair ones left the school with a few plastic dingdongs in their pockets. Trembling and fearful, they deposited them here and there, as cautiously as though they were handling dynamite. Then they planted them furtively; and eventually they plucked up their courage.

Meanwhile, the cell of the Independence Party was giving weekly lessons in economics to prepare their militants for the offensive that would pluck the riches of Quebec out of the soft hands of the English and the snapping jaws of the Americans. Those who remembered how to write took copious, careful notes. The economist looked at their rugged faces and thought to himself that teaching these villagers rather resembled the august act of planting seed on the rocky soil of the village.

"If you want to sell you have to put a price on things. If something hasn't got a price it won't sell. French Canadians have never wanted to put a price on their work, on their wood, on their animals. This was the consequence of a religious culture that made them fear punishment in Heaven if they attached a value to their earthly goods. Consequently, strangers came and wrote down prices, after evaluating them according to their own criteria. Naturally they were looking for a personal profit. Every product has to have its price. A free man, a free country, is a man or a country that sets his own price for his products."

Oliva Beauchamp had a little plastic dingdong in his pocket. When he left the Independentist economics lesson, while others lit their pipes and cigarettes he presented the strange object.

"Wanna buy a dingdong? It's Japanese."

Arrache-Clou offered:

"I'll give you ten cents for it!"

Oliva Beauchamp had understood the economics lesson.

"A Japanese dingdong's worth at least two bucks."

He sold it for a dollar. The first dingdongs on the market sold at this price and sometimes for even more. Then when the Japanese dingdongs had invaded the village, the market slumped. Soon production was so high that they weren't sold, they were given away.

"I'm gonna ask that economics professor to explain what's going on here," Oliva Beauchamp promised himself.

"My brothers," said the Curé, fists pointing to Heaven, "you have participated in the commerce of the flesh. You have put a price on your children's sex, on the part of their bodies that God made in his own image, that's destined to extend the life of our gallant little pious and industrious people throughout history. You have profaned the instrument of our survival. You are as guilty as the people in the cities who traffic in flesh. I don't mean the butchers, I mean the fresh meat of our children who are selling body and soul to the people in the cities. Brothers, with your crude laughter you've sold the flesh of your own children."

The villagers' chins sank to their chests. Remorse weighed on them like a mountain. The snow would never be deep enough, the ice would never be cold enough, the wind would never be clear enough to purify the village. The parents of the small children, the skinny ones, the coughers, and the fair ones would walk in shame, tortured, eyes on the ground, invisible under the snow, where God was waiting for them. In spite of all the Aprils and Julys, the depths of their souls would retain a little of that winter they would remember when it was cold as remorse. The snow can conceal the entire land, but it could never bury that memory.

The earth was not proceeding towards its deliverance. Beneath the frozen earth the villagers did not feel the beating of a distant heart. And if they put their hands on their own chests . . . Their lives were sleeping, peaceful and smooth.

One day the snow fell onto the windows: it was long, like time that does not pass. The next day, the light was brilliant as ice: glances were broken against walls that were invisibly pure. Another day a letter arrived from Florida; people gathered around the colourful pictures of the sea, the hot sand, flowers and oranges: they thought they heard the wind singing in the palm trees. Another day there was a blizzard, angry winds roaring through the snow, shaking the roofs, sinking into the walls and wrapping the village in a furious cloud that concealed knives of ice: the winds were as frantic as flames condemned not to burn. When the storm had abated, mothers waited at their windows for the snow ploughs, fearing that their children, playing in the snow, would crawl inside the tunnels under the crust and be snapped up by the snow plough, rolled and buried in piles of snow that wouldn't melt till May.

A few years earlier a child on his way to school saw a hand sticking out of a snowpile. Laughing at the idea of surprising one of his friends hiding in the snow, the child climbed up on the snowbank, wily as an Indian, and grabbed the hand. But his little friend wasn't attached to it! His body had been chewed up by the spiral blades of the snow plough. On the days when they were waiting for the plough, mothers kept counting their children.

"Those machines don't have to go so fast! They drive them like they're crazy!"

"It'd cost more; them machines make more in an hour than you make in a week."

"Goddamn money! The good Lord goes away but the money's always around."

Another day, an unknown car appeared in the middle of the street, a new car that gleamed in the brand-new sun. Oliva Duquette had gone away in the fall before the leaves turned red and now he was coming back, as they said, from winter.

"When the men come back, spring can't be far away."

"Have a good winter?"

"There wasn't too many mosquitoes!"

The men laughed as hard as he had made his motor roar; he had already forgotten the winter. The snow had melted in his memory. The men wanted to think only of the spring and of the roll of bills in his pockets that would allow him to sail through the spring and summer and even into next fall.

The men who came back were a little like Monsieur Bourdage, the stranger with the white Cadillac who had bought drinks for all the customers in the Auberge, assuring them that the houses in the village were built on gold.

"Me, I dug, but I didn't find nothing. Not even worms."

And they began again to tell the story of the burning church, of the flames racing through the sky that howled like dogs, the story of Démeryse's miracle, and the Notary, whom they had heard laughing that night, and the story of the organ that sang in the ashes.

"We oughtta talk about the white Cadillac we ain't seen again too."

Transistors were screeching on every floor, in every cell; songs were bombarded by commercials. From one cell to the next shouts carried messages, exchanged jokes, growing to a roar as they circulated. Prisoner number 2786 no longer heard the pounding on the walls that transmitted secrets, nor the sound of pails clanking against the bars to mark the beat of the music pouring from a transistor in another cell or another floor. He no longer heard the carts rolling along, carrying barrels of soup, nor the whistles to attract the guards' attention nor the challenges or threats being shouted from one cell to another, nor the curses of a man trying to jostle time, which had come to a stop. He no longer heard the love words offered by rough honeyed voices to their quivering canaries. Number 2786 had grown deaf to the tumult of human distress, but the sound of the key in the lock of his cell made him start as though he could feel the point of a dagger in his back. It was Chôcu Choquette, the guard.

"You in a good mood, 2786?"

"I already told you: 2786 isn't a name for a man."

"You know I'd rather call you Monsieur Bourdage—or J. J."

"Let's keep our distance. With that bunch of keys you don't belong to the same social class as me."

"With your white Cadillacs—they're always white; is that some kind'a superstition?—you don't belong to the same club as me neither. I got a '58 Ford."

"You bring the cigars?"

Chôcu Choquette agreed to make purchases "outside" as the prisoners said: no alcohol or pills or drugs, but little purchases that didn't disturb his soul as he slept. 2786 was a gentleman. Chôcu Choquette talked about him to his wife, assuring her that he wouldn't be embarrassed to have him at his table on a special occasion like the Feast Day of Saint-Jean Baptiste. Chôcu Choquette, the guard, would like to talk with this prisoner, without his uniform. 2786 had stolen a Cadillac. He always stole Cadillacs, and they were always white. When you know how much those castle-cars cost, you suspect that anybody who owns one must have stolen something.

"What're you reading, 2786?"

"You asking for the authorities?"

"Don't blame me if you're a prisoner and I'm a guard. A guy does what he can. You think I asked the Governor to let me come and stick my nose in your books? Books as thick as that without a single goddam picture of a woman to rest a man's eyes. As a matter of fact it's better if you don't look at too many women's pictures. Some guys upstairs got their eyes all worn out from rubbing them up against the tits in those magazines."

"I'm reading, *Escaping is Child's Play When Monsieur Chôcu Choquette is Your Guard!*"

Chôcu Choquette was becoming impatient. He wished 2786 wouldn't always make fun of him. He'd have liked a little more respect. Maybe he didn't like the cigars?

"How's your cigar?"

"Just fine. I'll pay you back. My appreciation won't be smoke."

A smile spread across the face of the guard, who bowed to accept the compliment. Getting up authoritatively, he said:

"I gotta write down the names of all your books. That there one—reading's the hardest thing in the world."

"That one's called *Barnato, the King of Gold*. It was published in 1937, the year I came into the world. It's the story of a clown that used to pick up a few cents in bars and nightclubs and circuses. A few years later he was the world king of gold mines! There's guys like that. You were born a prison guard and you're gonna die a prison guard, looking at life through a keyhole. There's guys like you and then there's the others."

2786 inhaled the smoke of his cigar, tasted it, exhaled. A far-off dream drifted through the cell. Chôcu Choquette stiffened, impatient, and used his pencil aggressively, copying the titles of the books on the shelf.

"There's nothing more precious," he announced suddenly, "than being free. Free to go home after work, free to tell yourself you're free."

"That kind of freedom stinks worse than no freedom at all! That's the kind I don't want."

Chôcu Choquette decided it was better not to argue. Laboriously, squinting at his notebook or the row of books, he sweated as he recorded a thousand titles: Pierre Berton, *Klondike: The Last Great Gold Rush*; V. Forbin, *L'Or dans le monde*; C. Ruston Read, *What I Heard, Saw and Did at the Australian Gold Fields*; Elizabeth Page, *Wild Geese and Gold*; James A. MacGregor, *The Klondike Gold Rush Through Edmonton*; W. B. Haskell, *Two Years in the Klondike and Alaskan Goldfields*; H. Villard, *The Past and Present of Pike's Peak Gold Regions*; Lord Cecil, *Goldfields Diary*.

Chôcu Choquette suddenly stopped writing and pushed his cap back as though his head were suddenly boiling with some extraordinary intuition.

"Listen here, 2786, you got all these here books in English, you decided to learn English?"

"If you look at things coldly, it would appear that gold only answers people that talk English to it."

"Could be. I don't know an awful lot of French Canadians that's ever found gold."

"But I'm gonna find the French world that'll make the gold answer me."

2786 rolled his cigar between his people in the manner, or so Chôcu Choquette imagined, of an American millionaire.

"That means I'm gonna serve my sentence till the end and when I'm out of here I'm gonna buy two white Cadillacs if I want them, and I'm gonna pay back everybody I ever did any harm to in my goddamn life."

Chôcu Choquette took off his cap; his head was boiling because he'd just sniffed something.

"All them books, they talk about gold."

Until then 2786 had been sitting on his pallet; now he lay down and stretched, hands behind his head.

"When a woman makes a banquet she reads her cookbook. These here books are my cookbooks."

The guard's hand was trembling under his notebook; he wished he could write faster. The pen made pirouettes.

"Don't talk so fast. The Governor told me to write down what you say when you talk about your books. I ain't doing this because I like it. It's my job. But I don't want to get your story down wrong."

"You're okay. So's the Governor. When I get my white Cadillacs I'll come back and see you. Don't worry, this time they'll be paid for. Cash on the table!"

Without getting up from his pallet, 2786 held out a piece of paper to the guard, who read: Hochheimer, Albert: *Gold: Scourge of the People*. Paris, Buchet-Chastel, 1957.

"Ask the Governor to get me this book; it isn't in the library."

Then he lay down on his pallet again.

"If you aren't worried about giving me a little credit, how about getting me some better cigars too?"

"You're cooking up something."

This was an insult. 2786 jumped off his bed. The guard stepped back. He thought the prisoner was about to yell. He spoke gently:

"I want to wash my hands. I want to be clean. I want out of here."

"These here books are my cookbooks," the guard read, checking the accuracy of his report. "I'll remember that by heart."

J. J. Bourdage approached Chôcu Choquette who, with his guard's reflex, stepped back from the prisoner.

"I'd be happier if you didn't tell that to the Governor. It'll just bother him. Why don't you keep it to yourself? Just between you and me?"

The guard agreed and went out. Cap in hand, because his thoughts had turned to steam, he hurried off to the office of the prison Governor, putting his hat on when he opened the gates across the corridors, taking it off to walk, and finally putting it on at the next locked door. When the Governor received him, Chôcu Choquette announced:

"2786 is cured. I just hope he won't get rotten again by being in contact with the others . . . We've cured that man."

The Governor ordered drily:

"Give me your notes."

"He's planning some kind of trick. But I'll swear on a stack of Bibles as high as my shoulder it ain't a dirty trick."

He reported word for word what he remembered. A few minutes later, preceded by Chôcu Choquette and followed by two armed guards, 2786 was led to the Governor's office. It was the first time he had been given this honour.

"Monsieur le Gouverneur," he said, "your office is just as dark as mine."

The Governor wasn't pleased at the comparison. Would he reply with a reminder that the prisoner must show respect to the authority who represented Society? He chose to be human, simply human.

"I keep the drapes pulled because I don't like the bars on my windows. Do you like the bars on yours?"

"Frankly, those bars make me want to clear out. Do you ever feel like doing that?"

"Come, come! We're still a joker, Monsieur Bourdage, still making fun. Are we still sharp-witted? Do we still have a golden tongue?"

"Sorry, Monsieur le Gouverneur. I shouldn't'a, but I feel comfortable with you. Don't take it as an insult, Monsieur le Gouverneur. Prison does funny things to a man. You lose your sense of reality."

"Let's get down to the facts, Monsieur Bourdage. I have intercepted all your mail."

"That's your right, Monsieur le Gouverneur, and your duty."

"You know where these letters come from?"

"Probably not from my old mother, Monsieur le Gouverneur; it's hard for her to write from the graveyard."

"Monsieur Bourdage, I've intercepted these letters from the Department of Natural Resources, the Department of Mines, the Department of Land and Forests . . ."

"Ah!"

The Governor scattered the letters across his table, most of them voluminous, the flaps of the envelopes open.

"Me and the Minister, we're as close as that," said Bourdage, holding up his hand.

The Governor exhibited a package of letters taken from a drawer.

"I also intercepted these letters from New Bid Gold Mines, Magusi River Mines, Mattagami Lake Mines, Camino Gold Mines, Red Ruth Gold Mines, Holmer Gold Mines, James Bay Gold Mines . . ."

The governor dropped the large envelopes impartially onto the table.

"And there's more . . ."

He opened another drawer and took a bundle of envelopes, all thick, and decorated with colours and company symbols.

"What's the meaning of this?"

"I've decided to take the economic destiny of Quebec into my hands."

The Governor stood up, furious, insulted, his finger on the buzzer.

"2786, have you robbed a bank?"

"No, Monsieur le Gouverneur."

The Governor waved before his eyes the list of books Chôcu Choquette had noted.

"You got gold fever on your brain!"

"There's two kinds of people, Monsieur le Gouverneur: them that find it and them that don't."

The response from 2786 sent the Governor back to his chair.

"Do you swear you've never robbed a bank?"

"Monsieur le Gouverneur, if I'd robbed a bank I wouldn't be confessing it to you. But I haven't stolen nothing since the last white Cadillac that brought me here. You see, Monsieur le Gouverneur, God created gold for man, but it wasn't God that put it in the banks. He put it in the ground.

And the ground belongs to everybody—even you, Monsieur le Gouverneur."

The Governor gestured to him to leave.

When 2786 went back to his cell his bookshelf had been emptied. All the books about gold had been requisitioned.

In the weeks that followed, the books returned to the shelf, one at a time. Chôcu Choquette himself brought them back and replaced them. He said nothing. 2786 waited for him to speak. But Choquette couldn't tolerate silence very long. One night, he confided:

"All the Governor's doing is read your books about gold. He's gonna know more than you when he's done."

"The Governor could never know everything I do."

Chôcu Choquette held out a bouquet of cigars.

"You notice these cigars are a lot better than the last ones?"

"Sure I noticed. Even the Governor couldn't afford cigars like these! Thank you!"

2786 lined up the cigars on his little table.

"I'll really enjoy smoking these. Because they'll be my last ones."

"You don't want me to bring you any more?"

"No. They're the last ones I'm going to smoke. You know, I want to leave this place as clean as a rag that's spent a few months in the washing machine. There's a hell of a good life waiting for me outside. I want to be clean. If people did me little favours in jail I might get dirty. A little cigar you smuggled in to me, it seems like nothing, but the smoke from that one cigar can make things pretty dirty. I could be black with soot. And you too . . ."

"When I bring you cigars it isn't to get paid."

"You're giving them to me? The debt's wiped out. Thank you. Thank you. I won't forget. Thank you. But I don't want no more cigars. I want to be treated like everybody else. When we see each other outside we'll be able to look each other in the eye. Are you gonna want to see me, your prisoner?"

Chôcu Choquette coughed to conceal his emotion, and to provide an explanation for the tears that filled his eyes. He writhed in a coughing fit, then stroked the spines of the books on gold.

"Ever since you started reading these books you been different from the rest of them . . ."

"Everything in my life has been ruined, everything: my birth, because I was born into a family where the poverty crowded out the goodness; I ruined my youth; when you're damned in childhood you keep running into the devil the rest of your life . . . But there's one thing nobody's going to make me mess up: my rehabilitation."

Chôcu Choquette wanted to put a friendly hand on his shoulder, but his guard's reflex held him back. He went out of the cell. As though he were running away. When the door was closed and locked he wiped his eyes.

When the Governor heard the guard's moving report he couldn't hold back a tear. For months now, every morning in front of his mirror he'd felt like vomiting at the thought of going back to this prison of which he was Governor. Now his tear, filled with unexpected happiness, enclosed him in a soft light in the dark, barricaded corridor of his life. He lived behind bars, like the prisoners. The hours of his life conformed to the prison timetable. He was the only one of all the prisoners who didn't have the right to dream about escaping. But was there any other place in the world where he could be as useful to his fellow men as in this prison? His tears had the taste of happiness rediscovered. Change a hoodlum into a man: was that not the miracle he had accomplished?

That very evening Chôcu Choquette brought to the cell of 2786 all the books that hadn't been returned to him, as well as a big bag of letters from companies dealing in gold. 2786 asked him to wait while he scribbled a few words on a piece of paper for the Governor.

"To thank him for what he's done."

He wrote:

Monsieur le Gouverneur, thank you. When all prisoners are exposed to so much goodness they'll be better men. I know you've read all my books and letters: it's your job. But I warn you, there's a hidden message in my books and letters; there's a great piece of luck waiting on the horizon for me. If every prisoner had the same hope they'd be better men. Thank you, Monsieur le Gouverneur, for all your kindness that's helping me become a clean man.

2786 J. J. Bourdage

P. S. Be severe so I won't slip just before I reach my goal.

The guard unfolded the sheet of paper 2786 held out to him, read the message, folded it again and slipped it into his pocket, from which he extracted a cigar.

"Want a cigar to celebrate?"

"No, I'm not smoking any more of your cigars."

"The Gospels say we should share . . ."

He broke a cigar in two and presented one piece to 2786.

"No."

Chôcu Choquette lit his half and smoked in silence. 2786 was staring into space. He was looking at his books, but the guard suspected he saw something further away.

"You ever think about gold?" 2786 asked.

"Yeah, I gave it a thought once when I went to the dentist to get a tooth fixed, this here big one . . ."

"If the world's rotten, it's gold that did it. But gold can save a man too."

The guard took off his cap. Trying to fix these words in his memory so he could report them to the Governor, and, at the same time, struggling to understand them, required a discernment that made his head boil. 2786, stared into the smoke and saw his shining dream.

"I just hope to God you ain't robbed a bank."

"There comes a time in the life of a man that's lived a little when he don't think as much about robbing banks as being robbed by them."

Chôcu Choquette pulled his cigar from his mouth.

"If you ain't robbed a bank then you found some gold, you lucky son of a bitch!"

"A clear conscience is as precious as gold. Before, I would'a robbed my father and mother if they'd had anything to steal. I've robbed my friends, I've robbed strangers. I've robbed the Government, even if that's no sin. I robbed night and day, I even dreamed about robbing. The only thing that was mine was my smell. Then all of a sudden I got my chance. I'll finish paying off society what I owe it and I'm gonna leave this place clean. I'm gonna leave and I'm gonna pay back everybody that helped me get clean."

"If I help you out," said Chôcu Choquette, "it ain't to get paid, it's to help you out."

"Don't talk like that; you remind me of my late father. He used to talk to me in that tone of voice when he was drunk. Papa, if you can hear me up there in Heaven, I want you to know you won't have to be ashamed of your child for much longer!"

For several days the soup had been inedible; grey broth, three grains of rice and two slices of carrot per barrel. Every day it looked more and more like meatless dishwater. Outside, though, there were no rumors of famine. The Board of Governors had decided to protest the soup. According to the bylaws of the Department of Justice (Prisons Section), prisoners were supposed to follow "normal channels," but the prisoners knew from experience that a coup was the only way to change the situation. One stroke of boldness and vegetables would be floating in the soup that very day!

The Board of Governors had perfected a strategy. Orders were communicated from cell to cell. No wall could prevent them from circulating. The prisoners were so absorbed in the preparations for the coup that the strictest discipline prevailed; with great enthusiasm the prisoners conformed to all regulations. Some of the guards were singing in the corridors. The good-natured ones, like Chôcu Choquette, declared that the prisoners were in a good mood; the pessimists, the grumblers, were convinced that the prisoners would make them pay dearly for these few moments of calm.

Every Thursday the prisoners lined up and went to the barber. There were several dozen chairs in the barber shop. The barbers were themselves prisoners: they gave up their razors without too much resistance. When the signal was given, then, several dozen prisoners would simultaneously be armed with razors. They would grab one guard and threaten him. The Board of Governors had selected the harmless Chôcu Choquette. The armed guard, up in his cage, wouldn't dare to fire for fear of wounding his colleague. And the Board of Governors designated Bourdage to lure his friend Chôcu into the trap.

During the obligatory walk around the outside courtyard, Bourdage whispered a message to his neighbour, asking him to convey it to the Board of Governors.

"My heart's with you, my friends, but my hands are tied. They watch me closer than the chaplain in a convent full of nuns. Through their spying they've found out I'm planning a personal coup."

"Your personal coup must smell pretty funny if they already got wind of it!"

"They searched my books and letters and they

know . . . Friends, if you get me into this it's like hanging a bell on a cat that's chasing a mouse! When the soup's good I'll be ready to give my share!"

A few hours later two armed guards came to take 2786 from his cell; he was summoned to the Governor's office.

"So," said the Governor, "it seems like I've found out you're planning some personal coup."

He looked 2786 in the eyes with assurance: he must have two revolvers in his pockets and his finger on the trigger to have such courage.

"Because you wanted to plan your personal coup quietly you refused to take part in the business with the barbers."

"Monsieur le Gouverneur, I want to get out of here clean. I want to follow the rules of this here prison like you follow your catechism."

"Did you ever read your catechism? Get out of here clean, you say? What you want to do is avoid surveillance, avoid suspicion, let your wardens fall asleep so there'll be general confidence for your personal coup. When a prisoner changes as much as you it's because he's planning a coup."

"Yes, Monsieur le Gouverneur, I'm planning a coup . . ."

Once again the Governor had the strength to look 2786 in the eye. J. J. Bourdage reminded himself that there were armed guards hidden behind the curtains.

"A personal coup, Monsieur le Gouverneur: I want to get myself hitched up to a clean life. You understand that? I'm gonna put on a new life like you put on a new, clean shirt, that smells new . . ."

"Is there any gold in your coup?" the Governor insinuated.

"Monsieur le Gouverneur, you know a lot more than you're letting on . . . You and me, we've read the same books."

"I started reading *Gold, Scourge of the Peoples*. Fascinating."

The next day, when the prisoners were exercising in the outer courtyard, they walked in twos, one behind the other, in step, tracing a circle that had to be perfect or the wardens' whistles would send out strident threats. 2786 found himself brutally squeezed by five prisoners—the two in front of him, the two behind and the one beside him. They smashed him with their elbows, feet and knees.

"You bastard, you're the one that spilled the beans to the pigs about the coup in the barber-shop!"

2786 whimpered. His words were cut off by blows. He lost his breath. He moaned, panting.

"Don't talk to me. Avoid me like the plague. They're watching me. If you say a word to me it's like telling a secret to the radio, from one Atlantic to the other. There's always somebody listening."

He was struck on the legs, in the belly and on the face; he fell to the ground under the boots of other prisoners who continued their circular walk. The guards waved their weapons and shouted. The prisoners picked up 2786. Their walk hadn't been interrupted.

"Stop talking to me, friends," said J. J. Bourdage, without anger. "Ever since they found out I'd struck it rich they won't let go of me."

"You struck it rich?"

The guards ordered them to speed up, The prisoners ran, their feet sliding over the gravel in the courtyard. The harsh noise was magnified by the enclosed space and the surrounding towers. After their walk, the prisoners were led back inside. 2786 barely had time to wash his scraped face with cold water, take off his boots and lie down on his pallet, when a key was inserted into the lock on his door, making an unbearable screeching sound.

"The Governor wants to talk to you," Chôcu Choquette announced.

A ring of keys was sparkling on a corner of the Governor's desk. Some force pushed 2786 towards the keys like a needle towards a magnet. He resisted. He wanted to avoid looking at the keys but his eyes wouldn't obey him. The Governor, smiling in his armchair, was smoking a cigarette with the happy look of God on the seventh day of the creation of the world. He offered the package of Players to his guest, holding it just above the keys. 2786 had to hold his hand just over the keys to pick up the cigarette.

"I know you stopped smoking but maybe here, in the intimacy of my office . . ."

"No thanks. I don't want no more smoke in my lungs. Don't want to get cancer. I want to live to a ripe old age. Old and clean."

"You're right. A man that's struck it rich wants to live for a long time."

"Live clean and outside. People won't be scared of getting dirty if they shake my hand."

"If every prisoner had just one clean idea there'd be a revolution in the jails."

"Everybody's got at least one clean idea, Monsieur le Gouverneur. But tell me: where does a clean idea get you nowadays?"

The Governor put his cigarete in the ashtray and chewed at his finger.

"Obviously, gold's a clean metal."

"Monsieur le Gouverneur, you're a public servant."

"Behind the public servant there's still a man. If you're scared of the public servant, sometimes it's a good idea to spill it out to the man."

Someone knocked. The Governor got up to open the door. His keys were on the corner of the desk. 2786 caught himself trying to pretend to forget about the keys. The prisoner grabbed his own right hand, the one that usually performed his professional tasks so faithfully, and wisely kept it from pouncing onto the ring of keys. The keys didn't move. The Governor whispered something briefly in the doorway, then came back and sat down. He wanted so much not to look at the corner of his desk, where the keys were, that he grimaced.

"I'd say it's healthy to spill the beans every now and then. My friend, a gold mine must be a hard thing for a single man to bear."

Instead of replying, 2786 glanced at the keys.

"Monsieur le Gouvernuer, you've tried to tempt me. Why? You know a man's weak when he's in jail, inside the walls."

The Governor found nothing to say. He looked at his prisoner. He no longer had the feeling of domination of a man who hasn't done wrong by a condemned man. He eyes weren't strong enough to bear the look of 2786. With a nod, he asked him to leave.

2786 walked along the corridors, head down, seemingly humiliated. When the other prisoners saw him they concluded that the pigs were keeping too close an eye on him. From his expression they guessed that he'd imparted no secrets. Hard as a rock, closed in on his secrets: that was how they saw him. They'd have to protect Bourdage. The Board of Governors warned the guards that Bourdage would be protected.

During the night he heard a noise at the door of his cell, but he didn't wake up. And without waking up he was pulled from his bed and stood on his feet. Hands clawed at his shoulders and arms, but he still slept. He was dragged like a sack through the corridors and down the stairs to the cellar. A cell door creaked, he was tossed onto a pallet, the door closed, clanging against the steel frame. Had he dreamed? The guards left, their feet gliding along the floor, the keyrings clinking at their belts, their big bellies heaving.

He never slept soundly. He knew he could hear the slightest hissing in the night. Was he dreaming? Where was he? He didn't recognize his bed. Where was he? He didn't recognize the walls. He didn't recognize his silence. Was he dreaming? When he heard a loud cry form in his chest and shoot out through the walls of stone and steel, he understood that he was afraid. His forehead was sticky with sweat. He yelled. He got up on his pallet and yelled even louder, as though he were trying, by shouting, to shove back the night that made him a prisoner even more than the stones. His voice was the voice of a desperate child. A light glowed at his door. Someone was looking through the peep-hole. Why had he yelled? Why was he afraid? He never yelled. He was never afraid. He started when the door opened. He was standing on his bed. Why was he shaking? Perhaps they'd put a tranquillizer in his food.

"The Governor wants you," said a guard he'd never seen.

The Guard, carrying his weapon, accompanied 2786 who was surprised to find himself shaking. The Governor, wearing a bathrobe, was sitting at his desk.

"You look all tired and upset. What's wrong? Don't you like your new apartment?" the Governor asked, rather mockingly.

2786 was silent.

"Your friends know you've struck it rich in some mysterious way. They think it's gold. You gotta be careful. Anything could happen to you. It's my duty to protect you."

2786 bowed his head. He was still shaking.

"There's no gold in my cell."

"You got gold on the brain . . . You've put your precious secret in the hands of people who have tortured the laws of society, but you should give it to a public servant that's concealing a man you hardly know."

"Monsieur le Gouverneur, a few years ago I was young, just getting started in business." (Was it the time for this story? He should wait till later. But he wanted to tell it tonight. Would he want to so urgently if they hadn't put tranquillizers in his soup? Would he remember the essential details?) "My boss told me, 'You got an education, you went to school with the priests, you know Latin, you're gonna go to Europe. With your education people won't take you for a goddamn savage. We won't be ashamed of you when you're with the Frenchmen in Marseille. If they don't understand your Canadian French maybe they'll understand your Latin.' I was supposed to take a suitcase to this guy in Marseille and bring back another one. The suitcase wasn't big, but it was heavy. When I was coming back in the plane with my suitcase under my seat because they'd told me to stay as close to that suitcase as if it was my wife . . ."

The Governor shrugged; he didn't want to be that close to his wife.

"There was a man beside me reading a book that was written in Greek, like I'd learned in school. 'Hey,' I asked him, 'you a Greek?' 'No,' the man answers me, 'I'm not Greek but if I could be born again I know what country I'd be born in: Greece.' The man closed his book and he put his hand on my arm: 'Young man, remember this all your life: the greatest happiness you can have will come from a woman. And the greatest unhappiness will come from a woman too.' He took his little white hand off my arm and snapped his fingers to call the hostess. He ordered champagne. We started drinking. He was on his way back from Greece. When he talked he practically had a Greek accent. His skin was as tanned as a pirate. He was a real Monsieur, but he was acting like a school-kid on holidays. He'd caught youth, the way you catch the flu. Or a sunstroke. He was a notary and he'd crawled out from under his papers like a cockroach. He was coming back from Greece with wings like a coloured butterfly. Champagne! More champagne! 'I've lived for fifty-two years,' he said, 'fifty-two years of a life that hasn't been any happier or unhappier than anybody else's. One thing about my job: for better or worse, your hands and your collar are always clean. Fifty-two years is a long time in a man's life. But I'm telling you, young man: open the door of this plane and I'd throw out those fifty-two years, without a parachute, right in the ocean, and hope they wouldn't remember me. I'm going to forget them. The only days I'm going to keep are the ones I've just lived!' Monsieur le Gouverneur, my glass kept being filled up with champagne before I even saw the bottom of it. It was like a spring; it just kept running. I thought about the suitcase under my seat. You know, like you see in the movies: a guy in a plane gets his neighbour drunk so he can steal his suitcase. I emptied my glass and I thought: this is the last drop I drink before I get both feet on the ground with my heavy little suitcase! When the Notary sees me take my glass away from the bottle he says: 'Aren't you drinking?' (He'd forgotten what I'd already had.) 'No,' I say, 'it's promise I made to my blessed mother on her deathbed. And a promise is a promise.' He says, 'A notary knows better than most people that your word of honour is your word of honour. You have to promise your dying mother something.' I remember that little notary's face of his in between the glass and the bottle he was holding, it started to scrunch up. Then he hollered: 'I don't want to die!' Me, I didn't know what to say. I thought he was scared the plane was going to crash. 'Apparently dying isn't any worse than going to sleep. A Greek said that in my grammar book.' Then the Notary asks me to listen to his story. He told me how he'd noticed a Greek girl sitting at a table in the sun, how he started talking to her and got her to go up to his room and into his bed. 'Love,' he tells me, 'is better than coming into the world. It's like going to Heaven.' He told me the story of his life. I know more about his life than if I'd read a seven-volume biography. And I'll remember some of the things he told me for a long time. 'In our country, everything's opposed to love. You can't love the frost that scrapes at your face, you can't love the snowstorms; you can't love the fall because winter's waiting at the other end and you can't love the land because there's too many rocks in it. And since there's no love in our rocky country, you dream about it. The country's opposed to love. If a man happens to fall in love he musn't let it show that he's got the wings of a bird, a heart like a whirlpool in the ocean and thoughts that embrace yesterday and tomorrow. He has to look as if he's picking up rocks. And with a look like that, every day the good Lord gives him weighs on him like a rock, and my goddamn notary's papers weigh even more.' 'Where are you from?' I ask him. 'From a land of hills and stones. The good Lord himself couldn't make a blade of grass grow on that land. We've been working our butts off for generations. It's so poor on top it must be very rich underneath.' 'Anybody ever go looking down below?' I ask him. 'The people that live there are so busy taking the stones out of the way of their plough they've never had the time, in ten generations, to see any farther than the handle of their ploughs. But for ten generations they've been telling themselves there was gold in their desolate land. It's like the idea of Heaven. Most people's lives are like our rocky land, dry and barren, but they believe in Heaven after death. For those people gold, like Heaven, is a legend that goes back, way back to the depths of night generations and generations ago. Myself, I discovered that, in my unconscious, I believe there's gold under the rocks just like the natives do, because I told my Greek love I come from a land of gold.' And I never forgot that either, Monsieur le Gouverneur."

"Where did the notary come from?" asked the Governor innocently, just as he might have asked what time it was.

2786 looked at him with a reassuring light in his eyes that said: I'm not falling into your trap.

"Monsieur le Gouverneur, there's some things I can't tell you yet."

He got up. Simpering, the public servant suggested that he not leave so quickly.

"So it isn't true about the gold? It's something he imagined? "

"Monsieur le Gouverneur, there's some things you don't invent."

"Monsieur Bourdage, I'm going to tell you something important that shouldn't be told in a place like the office of the Governor of a prison: after you're outside, as you put it, I'd like you to come to my house for supper some night, with my wife and even my kids. Just a family supper in my new house. Because I've just built my own house. When you spend your days behind bars like I do, it's nice to have a house where you're free. Comfortable. Of course, it's a little more than I can afford . . . Somebody that's interested in gold can understand the kind of risk I'm taking. When a midget thinks he's a giant, he's already stopped being a midget. You have to count on the future. This is a sincere invitation. The first Sunday you're outside."

"Don't talk to me like that, it's too human. I can't take it."

The Governor pressed a button and 2786 was taken to the "hole" as the prisoners had baptised the section reserved for dangerous criminals or those entitled to special protection. The next day, Chôcu Choquette brought a letter, a letter on official paper: "Under the terms of the law governing conditional liberations, and on the specific recommendation of the Minister of Justice of Quebec and under the surveillance of the Governor of this prison and following a special procedure proposed by the Deputy Minister of Social Welfare who will recommend it to the Minister of the same Ministry, detainee J. J. Bourdage is henceforth and immediately free, subject to good behaviour." 2786 could not hold back an oath that resounded through his cell, vibrated through the corridors, between the bars and made the statutes in the chapel tremble. An enthusiastic oath! The warden gave him another letter: it was an invitation from the Governor to have supper in his new house that very night.

"You and I prove that a man like you and a man like me can be friends. And, by way of a little joke, I would add that friendship is golden."

III

It is spring and harmony reigns between heaven and earth. Liberated from winter, life is quivering in the grass and beneath the bark of trees, in the plumage of birds and under the stones. The villagers look at the new blue of the sky and the sun obliterates their memories of ice and snow.

The green mountain is coming closer to J. J. Bourdage, its little houses dotting the greenery as the stones dot the fields. He leans against the warm shoulder of spring. This land, freed from the winter, and he, free from walls and iron bars, experience the same joy: a profound joy, wordless, sings in both of them. The sun's shoulder beside him is so real that he catches himself saying that the mountain is pregnant and will soon give birth to a marvellous little golden mouse. He bursts out laughing. And his white Cadillac seems to be laughing too.

Rings gleam on his fingers. The sunbeams of May leap nimbly from stone to stone. His hand grips the steering wheel. A feeling of power vibrates through J. J. Bourdage as though he himself was producing the light, as though the limpid light of this day came from his body rubbing against the spring. His body is a violin stirred by bright waves. He steps on the accelerator and sings. The countryside is even more transparent.

The first time he came to this country, this far-off village whose name is often forgotten by the maps of Quebec, J. J. Bourdage wanted to see again the man he'd met one day on a plane; he particularly wanted to find the house, the windows, the doors of that love-maddened man. J. J.

Bourdage had never been that much in love, not even when he was sixteen. The notary had sought love as Bourdage was seeking a fortune. The little man with skin the colour of a will had smuggled love home with him on the plane. The Notary had given everything he'd accumulated in a lifetime of pens scratching paper for the love he had found. An apple tree considered dead that suddenly burst into blossom: that was what the Notary had become.

The Notary had spent his life saving his own and other people's property, cutting corners, predicting the worst, and suddenly he was ready to give everything away for the girl he loved: his savings, his bonds, his debentures, his drafts—even his coupons. The Notary had waxed eloquent about the great people, the small nation, that had invented love, liberty and a religion that buried the dead as though they were still alive; and as the light he'd brought back from that land still blazed in the little man's eyes, J. J. Bourdage was thinking that this man who had never loved a woman before must have loved money very much. He thought of the notary's savings, his bonds, his debentures, his savings certificates, his investment certificates: all that wealth was waiting for a burglar just as the little notary had been hoping for love. He decided to steal them. The Notary wouldn't suffer too much because he was in love. His mind made up, J. J. Bourdage accepted a cigar, but refused the Notary's champagne.

"If the land in the village is even poorer than the people, why do they stay there?" The Notary asked. "We aren't a race of people that give up. Especially when we're wrong, we don't give up. That's our way of being right. We have an old saying that goes: 'In poor ground there's often wealth!' "

For a long moment the Notary smoked in silence. Then suddenly:

"But love is a great treasure, young man!"

The plane landed. J. J. Bourdage took his precious suitcase from under the seat. He prayed to God that the customs officers wouldn't be too curious.

"Yes, young man, love's a great treasure, but a man must always steal it."

Once the suitcase had arrived at its destination, J. J. Bourdage was invited by big hairy hands squeezing his shoulders to "lay low for a while." He had shown proof of his resourcefulness, determination, cold-bloodedness and ambition. All that had seduced his bosses who considered entrusting him with bigger jobs. Later. For the moment, he must at all costs avoid attracting attention. The men with the big hairy fingers who squeezed the bones and the muscles of his shoulders to express warm virile friendship suggested to J. J. Bourdage that he apply for a job at a savings bank: that way they'd know where to find him when they needed his services, later. The big fingers wrote letters of reference for him of a kind the head of the bank had probably never seen before. He took his place behind the wicket and the little drawer where he stacked banknotes that seemed to belong to no one.

The days were as long as weeks. One Friday after the bank had closed he was sure he was going to suffocate for lack of air; the only possible salvation was to try an adventure. Far away, in a little village, banknotes were waiting for him, and savings bonds and debentures. That night he drove calmly through the streets far from the bank, looking for a suitable car. He spotted a '58 white Valiant. When it was dark enough he slipped under the hood to start the motor. He drove out of town. He opened the windows. As he drove on, the air smelled less bad. The pure air made him cough. Very late at night, almost at dawn, he reached the village beside a road that had been traced along a rabbit path, between the rocks and knolls and spruce trees. All was night: the windows, the walls and the street—the single street. All was black as night. J. J. Bourdage had travelled to foreign countries but he'd never gone as far as to this village. And never had he been so close to the Notary's banknotes and savings bonds and coupons and certificates.

Suddenly the night was torn open and a light struck him in the face like a stone.

"What're you doing in my flowers?"

"It's as dark as the devil's asshole. If that's the kind of place where flowers grow!"

"Get out, you wretched man! You're not only stomping on my flowers, you treading on the flowers of fine speech."

The light pricked at J. J. Bourdage's eyes.

"Sorry I messed up your flowers, but I can't see the goddamn things!"

"But I know you, young man!"

The light moved away, leaving his eyes raw and scraped, and shone on a narrow, white face that looked like a sick fish in the dark waters.

"I know you young man, we travelled in an airplane together."

J. J. Bourdage wouldn't have been more surprised if he'd dived to the bottom of a dark well in his white Cadillac. He had to find a strategy, give a fast answer: "You're wrong, Monsieur, the only planes I ever saw close up were on the TV with my girl." Or: "I haven't forgotten the trip, Monsieur. I wanted to see you again. I've been looking for you."

Finally, J. J. Bourdage replied:

"You recognized me right away, in the middle of the night?"

"Come inside, young man, come in."

J. J. Bourdage followed the small black shape that moved with calculated steps inside the trembling circle of light. With a weak, insistent hand the Notary pushed him into his office. Books covered the walls. Big books in brown bindings. Behind the bare shiny work table, bigger than a refrigerator, was a black safe where all the debentures and bonds and savings certificates and wads of banknotes were probably asleep.

"It'd take a lot of noise to bust that safe; you'd hear it in the Old Countries!"

Once again the Notary began to recount his journey like a person who has repeated the same story a hundred times, with the same words, the same voice, the same silences. He had repeated it to himself a hundred times, in a low voice so as not to be heard outside the walls of his office.

J. J. Bourdage had struggled for hours to follow the road that tried to hide in the night. Now, exhausted, he tried not to fall asleep, to keep his eyes open, and he looked at the doors of the safe, with the wheel in the right-hand door, a sort of steering wheel that could lead him to the treasure. In a soft voice, with soft gestures, the Notary was telling him how one day he had seen love "in person."

"When a man's on earth he needs and wants nothing but love, but we put up with every constraint except the constraints of love. One day, through a blessing from the gods, I met a girl who said to me: 'I'll take your love, and I'll give you mine.' "

"How come you knew what she was saying if she was talking Greek? Maybe she was asking where the can was?"

The vulgar words irritated the Notary, but life had

taught him that he who bears a treasure must be prepared to be spat at.

"Love, young man, existed among men and animals long before the invention of language. Language brought wars and squabbling and insults and misunderstandings, all things that stand in the way of love."

The Notary walked over to his safe, turned the wheel in the right-hand door once, twice, three times: then he turned it in the other direction twice, then a half turn, then one turn to the left and another quarter-turn and the door opened. He took out a package of letters with brightly coloured stamps and spread them over the table.

"I don't understand her language but she knows mine and (taking from the safe a pile of books on which J. J. Bourdage recognized some Greek letters) I'm learning hers. Yes, Monsieur, I'm learning her language. Love means wanting to speak the same language."

The road was rubbing against J. J. Bourdage's pupils like an endless belt that was threatening to break down in the night.

"I suspect that you don't love, young man, But I, I love. If someone asked me to answer the question in the catechism: 'Why were you put on earth?' I'd answer: 'To love.' And, Monsieur, it's not a question of loving money, of loving alcohol or gambling: it's a question of loving a woman!"

His visitor was not worthy of looking any longer at the brightly coloured stamps or the books; he put them away in the safe, closed the door and turned the wheel like the steering wheel of a car.

"No, Monsieur, beside these letters and books nothing in that safe is worth as much as a single ray of love illuminating the face of a woman who is loved. And what about you young man: why do you not love?"

J. J. Bourdage kept himself from yawning to say:

"I love—I love life, in general."

"I lived for years without knowing what a fire, a sea, a sky, what freedom love was! My life was as closed-in as the earth in this country. This morning, young man, you will see the earth, you'll see tufts of sparse grass growing between the stones, you'll see the thin beasts that are inadequately fed by this land, you'll see that this land isn't exactly a desert, but it has no oasis either. Before I loved, my life was like the soil of my country. Yes, young man, my life was barren. I was waiting for death to stretch me out on this barren land. But young man, life is more marvellous than that! And to explain, I'll tell you one of the beliefs of this country.

"For generations the men and beasts of this country have been bent over in prayer, imploring the land to feed them: bent over and submissive. And the land never answered them. Yes, young man, for generations the men of this country have turned over and over again this earth which is as poor as their fathers and grandfathers. Do you understand why the people have struggled so stubbornly? They believe, young man, that when the land is cleared of all the stones, when all the rocks have been gathered, they believe this land will be rich. Yes, young man, the people who live in this country think they'll find gold under the stones."

J. J. Bourdage found himself on his feet, awake; the last words had rung out like bells pealing at a birth.

"Gold under the stone?" he repeated, incredulous.

"Don't think, young man, that the inhabitants of this country are gold-diggers. But there's a popular belief here: one day someone will split a rock and gold will pour out of it like blood spouting out of a pig."

"Gold under the rocks . . ."

"Yes, young man, and my whole life resembles the land of this country. Without knowing it, I was living like its inhabitants, hoping there would be gold under the rocks of my life. I probably believed it: how else could I have lived? But I notice that I haven't offered you anything to drink, young man. Would you like some coffee?"

"Monsieur le Notaire, you say that all the inhabitants keep their eyes on their ploughshares in case they see some loose gold?"

"Yes, Monsieur, for generations. Unfortunately, gold isn't eternal like love. The body dies but the soul continues to love in the centuries to come. Isn't it a finer thing to go on loving after death than to love in the countries of life?"

"Do you think there's gold under the stones?"

"If there wasn't any gold what would be the use of the stones?"

"Maybe you imagined . . ."

"Young man—but I haven't offered you anything to drink!—when they see their hill with the bedrock that comes through the grass, when they see the rocks moving through the fields like icebergs, the people dream of hidden gold: they talk about it among themselves, as a joke."

"Are they looking for gold?"

"No, Monsieur, they believe in it. That's enough. Look for gold? They'd be afraid of spoiling their dream. Believing it is more important than possessing, isn't it? when you possess nothing?"

The Notary's voice in the night sounded like a pen scratching a piece of paper. The years would follow the years and the strange gold in this story would still shine in J. J. Bourdage's memory. Once again, he told it to himself. As he emerged from his memories he saw the sun shining on the hood of his white Cadillac and on the stones in his ring and in the fields, on the grass and the rocks. He laughed.

"Gold! Gold! Gold!"

A few days before he'd had supper with the Governor of the prison on a new tablecloth on a new table on the new carpet in his new house, across from his wife who, under her smiling makeup, was as sour as a witch. When Madame was silent, when she stopped talking about how her husband, at night, studied books that would help him understand his "bandits"—"Sorry, his protégés"—the Governor tried to explain "an important reality it's essential to know": the onerous price an honest man must pay to have a roof built.

"Jesus Christ didn't have a stone to lay his head on, but the sky belonged to him, whereas in my case, my kingdom's a humble prison, just like you my friend. Now we're both on the same side of the wall, we could fraternize, couldn't we? Isn't friendship a shared treasure?"

The prison Governor tried all sorts of tricks to find out more about J. J. Bourdage's next undertaking. Supper ended very late. The Governor was a little tight. Madame excused herself, humiliated to see her husband drinking and laughing in the company of a dubious character with a police record. Alone, the men downed several *digestifs*. Then, walking carefully across his new carpet, the Governor showed J. J. Bourdage out, placing a protective arm around his shoulder. Opening the door:

"Freedom is there, ahead. Walk straight ahead, that's the road to dignity."

Before he set out, J. J. Bourdage turned around.

"Monsieur le Gouverneur, do you believe in the superstitions the old people passed on to their children, from generation to generation, for many many years?"

"Yes, that's what makes up a people's culture. You have to believe in it."

J. J. Bourdage held out his hand. Touching the soft hand of an honest man reminded him of an unpleasant sensation, when as a child on an uncle's farm he had touched a cow's teat.

"Thanks, Monsieur le Gouverneur; I won't forget it's thanks to you that I'm clean now. Thank you."

He turned his back. The Governor shouted at him from the door:

"My door's always open to you. When you build a house that costs as much as this one, that ruins you as a matter of fact, the door has to be open. *Au revoir*, my friend. See you soon! and good luck!"

The gravel creaked when he walked on it. J. J. Bourdage shouted to the Governor who was standing in front of his new house, all lit up like a saint in his niche in the church:

"You're my real father. I owe you my life."

"When you get your gold don't forget your friend in his new house that's ruining him."

And the Governor, that distinguished man, let out a laugh whose force and straightforwardness surprised him. The laugh resounded in the night as though the Governor had said: "Gold! Gold! Gold!"

And the echo repeated it.

Abruptly, as though it had run into a wall, the white Cadillac screeched to a stop. J. J. Bourdage jumped out to see a little mound of ashes, blackened bricks, burned beams and perforated sections of walls. Old people were talking, gesticulating, probably trying to bring the past to light, to rebuild the demolished church through their words.

"That the church?" he asked.

"It burned down."

"The fire got everything, even my upholstered prie-Dieu."

"And now we ain't even got a place for our own funerals."

"A man without a church, he's a man without a house."

"At our age, a man without a house, he's like an old shadow bent in two, wandering through the village. Not a man."

"That there church was made of bricks and stones, but

it burned up like tobacco."

"How'd it happen?"

"Some crazy youngsters were hunting for gold in the ground: they opened it up and what do you think came out? No fortune, no gold. Hellfire, that's what came out."

"Gotta open up the ground for planting, not for hunting fortunes."

"Hunger for gold don't run in our blood."

"Shouldn't open up the ground to rob from the dead."

"We got work in our blood; gold ain't work."

"After they opened up the ground the dead people came out and set fire to the church, and then when the church was just a pile of ashes they sprinkled some on their heads and went back home."

"When they run out of dead people under the ground it's the living that pay."

"You should set your sights on Heaven, not the ground!"

J. J. Bourdage got back in his white Cadillac. He shouted to the old men through the window:

"All you have to do is bend over a little: you'd pick up enough gold to build yourselves a gold church and gold coffins and you could use the leftovers for gold embroidery on the Curé's chasuble. All you gotta do is bend over."

The eyes in these old bodies, bent to the ground by painful labour and old age, eyes that were used to looking up to the sky where God awaited them, glanced at the ground; they didn't think about gold but about the sleep that awaited them. The grey notion of death passed through their tired eyes. J. J. Bourdage was already somewhere else.

The white Cadillac had bounded off to the presbytery.

"Monsieur le Curé, I'm starting up a Big Deal in this village. Don't give your burned-out church another thought; if the good Lord keeps me safe and sound I'll be able to rebuild it for you. And I'll put gold leaf wherever you want it—on the ceiling, on the statues."

"Just what sort of business venture is this, my son?"

"Monsieur le Curé, I'm gonna ask you to keep silent about the promise I made you and (getting to his knees, head bowed like a dog expecting to be patted) I also ask for your blessing."

The Curé muttered something in Latin and traced a cross above J. J. Bourdage's head.

When the owner of the Auberge du Bon Boire spotted J. J. Bourdage he stood still, hesitant, busily trying to tie together past and present.

"You goddamn thief," shouted the Aubergiste, charging at J. J. Bourdage with fist outstretched, "the only reason I didn't send the police after you was because I know a thief always comes back to the scene of the crime."

J. J. Bourdage turned his back on his attacker and announced with a laugh:

"Mademoiselle, drinks for everybody! And don't forget the boss!"

The Aubergiste pounded his fist on the counter.

"So you didn't forget me, eh Boss?" said J. J. Bourdage. "That does my heart good."

He spread his arms as though expecting the Aubergiste to rush forward and embrace him.

He was grumbling though, fists clenched.

"You come back to pay your debts, you goddamn thief?"

"An honest citizen doesn't mind being called a thief by an innkeeper that waters his whisky!"

"If you show the teeth you got left around here, I'm gonna bust them in."

"Poor Boss," said J. J. Bourdage with his brightest smile, "what prison are you getting out of, you're so foul-mouthed? Better watch your language, or people'll think your Auberge is a dump!"

"I'll talk polite to you when you're polite enough to pay last year's bill."

"What! The Company always pays my hotel bills the week after I leave. Hang on. I just left a big hotel where I spent a few weeks. The Company's already paid my expenses."

"Your goddamn Company didn't send me a single goddamn cent!"

"Those goddamn capitalists, always exploiting little guys like you and me. Where's the phone?"

Angrily, J. J. Bourdage picked up the phone.

"Operator, I want Dallas, Texas, right away. Emergency. Collect, reverse the charges, *frais virées* . . . It's Texas Gold Mining I want, the number's 876-3281. Hello? This is Bourdage speaking. Give me the Travel Expenses Department."

He began to vociferate, red, yelling even louder.

As he was speaking English, the drinkers at the table didn't understand what he was saying, but when they heard him yelling so loud–and in English–they could guess that this was an important man. The proof that he was very important came when the bottles he was paying for arrived on their tables. J. J. Bourdage hung up. He kept his eyes lowered for a moment, bent over in his rage. then he looked up, silent.

"Maybe I was a little hard on you," said the Aubergiste, "but in this business credit can ruin you. People drink more than they can pay for."

"The Company can pay and it's going to pay!"

"I'd like to offer you a drink to help you digest the stupid things I said," the Aubergiste offered.

"I'll gladly accept a drink, but it's the Company that's going to pay for it, just like the others!" (Wiping his forehead) "Today, the Company's like a car that doesn't want to go under a hundred miles an hour."

The Aubergiste looked through his bottles, remembering J. J. Bourdage's favourite brand.

"Ah, business is tough, real tough. And you can't trust nobody. People aren't religious anymore."

"Business is tough and you have to be even tougher if you want to make it. Your health, Boss!"

"Welcome to the Auberge!"

How could the Aubergiste, who had listened to the phone call, suspect that J. J. Bourdage hadn't called Dallas? He hadn't even spoken to the operator; he hadn't even dialed 0. He had been shouting into a deafmute telephone receiver.

"This summer," said the businessman, "I got more than when I left. I need a whole floor in your Auberge. Temporary. While I'm waiting to buy the Auberge for my head office."

"Rent a whole floor?"

"Yes. I'm starting a Big Deal."

"Buy my Auberge?"

"Boss, this is the start of a Big Deal."

On the stage, at the microphone, a singer–male or female?–in a sequinned costume, wrapped in the pink and orange light like furs, meowed a song of a cat craving a tom. When the number was over J. J. Bourdage walked through the applause and quite naturally picked up the microphone.

"I ain't no singer. My name's J. J. Bourdage. I'm a businessman. I'm saying it in English because if you say *homme d'affaires* it don't seem as if you're making as much money! I'm the one that bought the first round. And I'm starting up a Big Deal so I'm gonna buy the second round too. I advise you to drink beer. When the Big Deal's in the works we'll drink champagne. And when that time comes you'll all be real glad to buy the champagne for me. Now, I'm going to ask you to tell everybody that's got land beside the Famine River—yes, everybody that's got the Famine River running through their land—to come and see me here at the Auberge, tomorrow, if they want the Big Deal to be their Big Deal too. And while you're waiting, don't drink too much—just enough to keep the Boss alive! Keep your thirst for the Big Deal!"

The applause was longer and more enthusiastic than for the androgynous singer. The image of prison came back to him—the refectory with its gray walls, and the prisoners banging their metal cups against their metal plates.

"Boss, if there's anybody in any of the rooms on my floor you'll have to kick them out."

"Yes, Monsieur, we'll empty the place. But is your Big Deal guaranteed honest? I don't want nothing dishonest in my Auberge."

"The Company obeys all the laws of the economy and international finance."

The next day, well before noon, the farmers were heading for the Auberge, suspicious, their shirts burned by the sun and dried earth clinging to their boots. The Aubergiste offered them drinks.

"It's on the Company. The one that's behind the Big Deal."

The farmers hesitated.

"We just come to see what was going on. Anytime we got a present it was from somebody that was trying to screw us."

"You don't trust the hunk of cheese in a rat trap."

They weren't in the habit of stopping work in the middle of the day and coming to the Auberge to drink beer. The day had been created for work. Not being in the fields worrying the soil, that intractable beast, was a waste of the fine light of day. The farmers grumbled and smoked, hesitating to drink. The Aubergiste had been ordered not to tolerate an empty glass. Through the smoke from pipes, cigars and cigarettes rolled by big earthy fingers, he kept repeating:

"When you go into a Big Deal you gotta celebrate the start of it."

"Who's paying for this?"

"The Company."

"A Company don't get rich buying beer for honest farmers. There's something fishy here."

"The Company's better off paying for our drinks than spending its money on taxes for the government."

"If the Big Deal starts with beer I wonder where it'll end?"

"There's a snake hiding in the grass."

Hands went into pants pockets to check that the flap on the billfold was buttoned, and the chain holding the billfold fastened to the belt.

J. J. Bourdage came in, wearing his broad-brimmed white hat.

The farmers had seen that kind of hat on television, on the heads of Western singers. A hat as white as his white Cadillac, and just as big. He was carrying a briefcase and wearing a number of rings.

"Messieurs, I invited you here because the Company needs you. It wants to ask you for something."

"This ain't the first time we got screwed by a Company, but it's the first time they gave us any warning!"

"The Company don't like doing business with spineless simpleminded men that get screwed. The Company likes tough customers that don't get screwed, that are ambitious to make money! That's the kind of man we like. And those are the people I'm going to talk to today. The rest of you can go and get screwed somewhere else! I just want to talk to you if the Famine River runs through your land. And I just want to talk to the men. To the women I say: the Company's strong, but it ain't tough enough to take on women!"

Hearty laughter poured through the room, then heads began to turn—whispers, laughter, denunciations. "Hey, the Famine's a mile from your land." Protests: "The Famine goes right through the middle of my bran, just as clear as the crack in your bum." Jokes: "The Famine goes just under my cow when she's standing still." Accusations: "You ain't even got any land!" When calm was restored J. J. Bourdage began again.

"The Company's asking you to give me the right of passage on the Famine River where it touches your land."

"You gonna come by very often?"

"You coming by boat or bulldozer, on foot or on horseback?"

"How many times?"

"If you agree to give the Company rights of passage, write your name on this form I'm handing out. Those are the people I'll be dealing with, the ones with no risk. As for the rest of you, anybody that's hesitating, we could give them time to go and ask their wives' permission. Read the form before you sign it. I ain't gonna screw you. Don't shut your eyes; you aren't taking communion—this is business."

The farmers read the form. And they looked at one another, questioning.

"This here's the first time anybody asked permission to go in the Famine River."

"You gotta watch out when somebody asks permission."

Hesitations. Reflection. Finally they all signed the form. Satisfied, J. J. Bourdage carefully checked the dates and signatures, the crude handwriting of diligent but ungifted schoolboys. He put the forms in his briefcase and snapped it shut. Irrevocably.

"Gentlemen, you've just given me exclusive rights of passage on the Famine River which flows through your land. That means that for example if I find gold, like it's happened in the West, I get to keep any gold I find."

The farmers leaped up, protested, stamped and threatened: furious bulls around J. J. Bourdage.

"The Company don't want to screw you, it wants you to be its associates in a profitable venture according to studies carried out by our experts. The Company wants associates, not victims. Associates that like risks the way it does. Gentlemen, you don't build a fortune with money, you build it with risks. Risks! Reasonable risks! Who was it that said French-Canadian *habitants* aren't reasonable?"

Slowly the farmers calmed down.

"The Company's offering to make you associates in our Big Deal. Do you want to become associates in the Company?"

"We know what you have to do to get into Heaven, but how do you get into a Company?"

"I suggest you invest fifty bucks. That's for the partnership."

"What does partnership mean in French-Canadian?"

"It's a word that don't exist in French-Canadian because we're always customers, never partners! But things are changing! And it's companies like the Company that are making these changes happen. Now you've put in fifty bucks. That gives you the right to get all the information the Company puts together, after it does an in-depth study of the soil, which, according to certain fundamental but incomplete studies, could contain gold ore. You'll be given a map with all the details pertaining to the shores of the river, or what we call in educated language, the anomalies of the geological conformation. There'll be little crosses to show where the gold's hidden. And I repeat, I emphasize, you'll all get a detailed map of your land showing the detailed study of the shores of the Famine. I repeat: your neighbour won't know, he won't see nothing except his own copy. I'm being frank. If we don't find gold on the shores of your land, you'll lose your fifty bucks."

Chou Racine got up.

"To hell with our fifty bucks if we find a treasure!"

Another farmer, Thomas Boucher, the Seamstress's husband, raised his hand to speak; he had a certain authority because the din of arguments and wishes stopped.

"You been talking about shores. Shores here, shores there. But I'm telling you, if you're looking for love you don't just tickle the edge of the lace on her slip. No sir, you'll try and go farther, at least I hope so. Always, that's how we do things here: go farther. If you're hunting for gold how come you're satisfied with just tickling the shores of the Famine? How come the Company turns up its nose at the idea of going inside our land?"

"I'm being frank. I'm not hiding the fact that the Company wants to get rich. If each of you gives me five thousand bucks, well then we'll dig in your land, we'll turn it all upside down and we'll pull that gold out like a scared groundhog. Is there anybody in this room that wants to risk five thousand bucks?"

The farmers dared not look at one another to avoid seeing their own impotence reflected in the others' eyes. They lowered their heads. J. J. Bourdage let the silence spread, then:

"The trouble with French Canadians is they always stop in the middle of things. I don't understand how come we even manage to make such big families!"

Laughter rose from bellies to chests, and burst out on the faces of the farmers who came back to life. They raised their heads.

"Nobody here's ready to risk five thousand bucks. Nobody but the Company's going to invest five thousand bucks on the land that belongs to each and every one of you. On one condition: you risk ten percent of that five thousand bucks out of your own pockets. The Company'll invest that. It's a kind of moral guarantee. But I'm being frank: if we find gold you lose your deposit."

"And what if you don't find none?" worried a farmer who spat out some tobacco as he spoke.

"A company like the Company operates so it won't lose money. If by some bad luck—and that would be contrary to our preliminary studies—if by some stroke of bad luck there ain't no gold here, the five hundred bucks you've invested—that is, the ten percent of the Company's five thousand bucks—would be converted into two thousand five hundred—yes, two thousand five hundred—preferred shares in a mine that will be opened in the area, in a place I can't name because I want to avoid speculation. Not far from here. Gold mines are like weeds: once you find one somewhere they spread."

"How come," asked Thomas Boucher, the Seamstress's husband, "how come you ain't sticking to the formula: dig now, pay later?"

"With respect to my five thousand bucks, your ten percent's a small moral guarantee; you agree not to harm the Company's work, either directly or through an intermediary. Once there was a woman in Rouyn that wouldn't let us dig in her garden, underneath her cucumber patch. The Company dug in spite of the lady. She brought us to trial. And believe it or not, the Company found enough gold under that lady's cucumbers to buy up the Government of Quebec. The Company don't want to screw you. Here's the forms to sign. (He handed them out to everyone.) Sign the form, sign the special cheque. Remember now: when you invest you open up your socks to let the money in! I'm being frank. You lose five hundred bucks if we find gold. Read every line on the form, even the fine print."

The farmers read. It took a considerable effort. They were silent and nervous. No one touched his pen to sign his name.

"There's something I can understand," said J. J. Bourdage very gently. "Today with this women's liberation a man that wants to be in style can't sign a cheque till he asks his wife's permission. The Company understands that. So do I. It's your God-given right. Those that want to, you can go and ask your wives' permission to sign a cheque. It's sad. I understand. It's a sign of the times."

Trembling, big earthy fingers seized pens, which began to scratch across the forms and the cheques.

"If you ain't scared of your wives, make your cheques out to J. J. Bourdage, official agent."

As soon as a cheque was signed, J. J. Bourdage picked it up. The forms piled high. All the farmers had placed their signatures on the forms and on the cheques. He ordered beer.

"I invite you to celebrate the beginning of a Big Deal with me. But before we get warmed up, there's two things I want to tell you. First, if you haven't got up the nerve to ask your wives' permission, do it anyway. The Company can wait. Nowadays with this damn female liberation it's better for a man to ask his wife's permission if he don't want to pay for it in bed! And second, if you're sorry you signed, there's still time. Some people, they're scared to take a risk and I understand that. It's only human to have cold feet. And money's something that should be made in happiness!"

Then J. J. Bourdage proclaimed:

"To your health! To the health of gold!"

He put the forms and cheques into his briefcase and closed it abruptly. Once again the time had come for J. J. Bourdage to make himself invisible.

He shouted out a warning.

"The Company wants you to keep quiet about this deal. If you've got a treasure in your house you aren't going to shout it from your rooftop."

Once again, he was to leave with something that belonged to other people. Once again his nerves were quivering: was it with pleasure or fear? He walked along the waxed dance floor, his feet sliding, his leg muscles as tense as though he were climbing onto a very high roof. The briefcase under his arm felt as heavy as a boulder. But he also felt the light sensation of a wing beating at his shoulder. He was ashamed of his sentimentality: he wanted to be like others, feeling nothing and giving himself up to his undertakings as imperturbably as an umbrella in the rain. As soon as his hand flicked something, all the muscles in his body quivered. He hated himself then. But he dreaded the day when his muscles would turn to string. Every time he undertook something, the same crazy ideas whirled through his head. He seized the telephone and shouted:

"Mademoiselle, this is J. J. Bourdage of the Company. Give me Dallas, Texas. Oui, Mademoiselle, Texas Gold Mining. Hello. Please give me Mr. Selwinburger. This is Mr. Bourdage. Hello Sel! This is J. J.!"

The farmers stopped drinking and grumbling to listen to him. The farmers listened to this strange language where there was nothing to understand.

"The Company's a big company that talks English!"

"I know what he said!" one of the farmers exclaimed. "He was asking for trucks and bulldozers."

"I ain't too crazy about them things crawling across my land."

"If it's a big Company . . . Big companies don't move around for minnows. If you ask me, they're gonna bite here."

"How come it's always big American companies that find out we got something valuable?"

"We got something valuable, but that don't help us live any higher off the hog."

J. J. Bourdage hung up, congratulating himself for his ingenuity: it didn't take a Leonardo da Vinci to press down the button and speak into a dead telephone. He walked over to the farmers.

"First of all," he shouted (he waited until it was quiet), "I'm offering everybody a round. It's the last one, because you mustn't drink too much. There's work to do before you make your fortune. Second, I'm going to work. My office'll be here at the Auberge. While I'm waiting for the Company to buy the Auberge—apparently it isn't for sale, but when the Company decides to buy . . . I'll be on the second floor. That's where you should send me your wives if they give you any trouble."

As he climbed the stairs J. J. Bourdage saw his broad-brimmed hat appear in the spotted mirror screwed to the wall, then he saw his face emerge and his shoulders. The image irritated him. He wanted to be seen by no one now.

Not even his own eyes. Already, he wanted to be somewhere else.

Now only the last stage of his undertaking was left: to flee. How he wanted to jump into the white Cadillac and make his getaway with a squealing of tires on the pavement! But he had to wait, not give the appearance of running away, not seem to be thinking of running away. Time was a motionless block in which everything was frozen and he was waiting in the midst of time, like an insect sealed inside a plastic cube. But he was alive! Drink. He picked up the telephone to order something. Then he hung up. He mustn't drink today. Once again, unmoving time. He lay down on the bed. He had spent so many hours of his life lying on a mattress, eyes open, watching time that didn't pass. He had, of course, examined the cheques. But had the farmers signed them properly? He got up, worried, to check. Several thousand dollars. He added them up: only seven thousand five hundred dollars. Why should the harvest be so meager, after all the work he'd put into his Big Deal? He couldn't even buy a new white Cadillac. Once again he'd be forced to borrow one. Always, he was preparing, planning, organizing some vast operation, but the returns were always small. Why was he condemned to Big Deals with small salaries? One day someone had told him: "You're using a lot of sail to catch a little fish." Where had he learned to dream such grand dreams? Why was he always inventing? Others picked what they saw before their eyes, within their reach, and their harvests were always fine. They had smaller sails but they caught more fish. What he really enjoyed was inventing, even more than gathering the fruits of his invention. But they had to be gathered!

A child, he looked out the window of the closet, looked out on the laneway, the grey wooden fences and the cluttered balconies, and he saw old men's heads, children's faces and then, in the distance, the mountain with its trees and castles hidden in the foliage. Sometimes he would see one of their towers. The castles were guarded by dogs, someone told him. One day he'd go walking under those trees, he'd tame the dogs, one day he'd walk right inside the castles. People who don't dream have better harvests. He'd have to stop dreaming. He had no future. He had no past. All he had was his dreams. Not to dream . . .

All around him men and women were stirring. Their

faces were yellow and covered with wrinkles. Like dried mud. They had been baked by the sun. Their clothes were dark and their smell wasn't a city smell. The women's faces were white; they were fat and they talked louder than their husbands. The only people they knew were people they'd never seen and when he heard them say their strange names he had to keep from laughing. These men and women had powerful voices. Usually they couldn't talk so loud because of the thin walls and the neighbours who listened to every word and then repeated it to the other neighbours. These men and women could only talk about people who were sick or dead. It seemed as if they didn't know anybody who was alive! They spoke about the wind, the rain, the winter, the oats that hadn't grown, the cow that had died giving birth to a calf that Arsène the butcher had saved, they talked about the horse with the broken leg and they talked about their misery, their misery, of the days that were too long, of the summer that didn't come, of the rain they kept waiting for, and of "always being harnessed to the land, working like horses: sometimes I wonder if God even loves us."

"And we're always waiting for the land to give us something to eat."

"And when we come to the month of the dead we don't even know if we're going to have enough to get through the winter."

"God didn't create this land for feeding people with, he made it to bury the dead, that's all."

"That's right, remember at Adrien Grussavoine's funeral?"

"Don't talk about him. If they'd'a opened up his body they would'a found a brain the size of a rabbit turd."

"Don't speak ill of the dead."

"What misery it is, life and death!"

"Why is it we stay here, on these same rocks, in these same houses, for generations and generations, just waiting?"

"If you ask me, I think we spend our whole lives digging our own graves."

"This land, it's something we should run away from, like the plague."

"When you're French-Canadian you can't go much further than the end of your own bit of land."

"There's some places where they find gold in the

ground; how come we never find nothing in our goddamn land?"

"Maybe we don't find nothing because we talk French to it."

"You throw a handful of seeds into this goddamn land and then three months afterwards you harvest a rock."

"We ought to just leave this land and get out of here."

"That's something you can say when you're sitting around having a smoke, but no, you can't do that."

In the cupboard the child who wasn't yet called J. J. Bourdage looked out at the wooden fences, the children who were prisoners inside the fences, the winding staircases, the grey balconies; he looked at the mountain with its castles hidden in the trees; he had never entered this foreign land.

"Some people left the land to come to the cities; I wonder if they're any better off here."

In the cupboard where piles of boxes bore the names of merchants from the old village, the child knew what would happen. These men and women were waiting for an answer from his father who had chosen to sow his days in the asphalt of the cities. They hoped he would tell him he'd made a mistake, that he'd admit he missed the old land. His father didn't answer. The child had never known if his father would rather have gone back to the land. His father never opened his mouth when the question was asked by uncles and aunts. Rather, he would get up and come and take refuge in the closet. He would stand at the window, black-nailed hands crossed behind his back, and silently stare at the criss-crossed fences and the tangled balconies and, in the distance, the mountain with its trees that hid the castles. What did he think about? Did he see the land where he had spent his childhood? He would bite his lips. To the questions of uncles and aunts he would reply within himself, in silence. And then his mother would say:

"You know, the city's as hard to work as the land."

And a woman in a flowered dress replied:

"When you get right down to it, if you work a piece of land, even if you don't harvest nothing you still got your land; but if you don't harvest nothing in town you ain't got a thing, not even a place to be buried."

His father would look out over the grey laneway, the fences, the battered walls, the poorly sealed joints, toward the mountain where the rich people lived, the rich who owned the city as others possessed a piece of land. They never came to his part of town and behind their dark windows they spoke English. His father was silent. The child was suffocating behind his father and the window. He coughed and went out.

Suddenly he threw a stone and broke a window. His arm plunged briskly into the star-shaped hole and his feverish fingers plucked out a watch. And another. And another. He took flight. He had dared. At last he had dared. He had been coming to this window for so many days, and going home empty-handed. He'd never had the courage to break the glass. And now he had dared. The watches on his arm were hidden by his shirt sleeve. The air in his lungs didn't taste the same. The buildings around him seemed less high. He had grown. He was tall now, high as a bird flying over the city, and he spat down on the men at a street corner, bent over in trenches, busily digging the dirt, men who resembled his father. They wouldn't forgive him for breaking a window, but they forgave themselves for their down-trodden lives, their noses stuck in the hard earth of the city. He would invent a name for himself. The old one would be abandoned to misfortune, which would devour it. He dreamed of a big car that would fly with a wail over the big brick houses pressed close together. No, he was no longer a child as he had been that day when fat white women in flowered dresses were at his father's house with their black-suited husbands; they spoke of the land and the dead. They only stopped talking all at once to let beer gurgle down their thick necks. When they laughed–rarely–the beer spurted out with their laughter, spattering the poorly mortared walls. Some man always said:

"Brother, if you told us the truth you'd admit that you howl every night because you miss the land."

"So does Annette; your wife misses the land. She must be as heavy as a rock in bed!"

"When the good Lord sowed all those rocks on our land he put them on our backs too."

"Sometimes, like they say sometimes, we're so hopeless we ain't got enough sadness to be sad."

"It seems like the good Lord gives his little sparrows everything they need, so some little sparrows must be better off than us."

"Little sparrows ain't got an appetite like yours."

The room filled with a fog of beer. All the men with their baked faces, and the round white women, burst out laughing, and it sounded like the crying of terrified animals. They stood, they danced, they laughed, they tapped their feet, they nudged one another, and their laughter shook the women's fat and made it quiver. The baked faces cracked. They laughed as though they were in pain. A billfold fell to the floor. The child swam through the swell of cries and laughter, picked up the object, left the room, went down the staircase that was buckling under its rot, he went down to the piece of ground where they were allowed to walk—a piece of ground as big as "a shovelful of dirt over a dead man," as one of his uncles said. The child sat on the bottom step, opened the billfold, counted the dollars—what a fortune!—he counted them again and put them back in the leather case. He dug a hole in the dusty hardened ground, put his treasure in it and covered it. Then he ran up the stairs and took refuge in the cupboard, where he had to stand on tiptoe to look out the window, a little higher than his eyes, towards the mountain. The men and women, faces strained with laughter, drank and danced and stamped for most of the night. When they went to sleep they fell. In the morning the child rushed to the staircase. The billfold was no longer in the hole. The child dug, dug under the bottom step. The billfold wasn't there. The child scratched at the dirt with all the strength in his fingernails. He dug all around with a dried branch, he picked and scratched.

"Looking for worms?"

"I'm looking . . ."

With his hands and a dry branch he dug in the ground for a long time. And for a long time his father watched him from the balcony.

"If you buried something you'll never dig long enough to find it; the Devil's pulled it down to his place."

"I'm digging for gold."

The stairs shook because his father stamped his foot on the balcony and now the words tumbled onto him with furious force. He bent his back under the blows.

"Gold! Gold! Crazy goddamn little fool! Our family's dug the ground for generations, from father to son—longer than you could dig even if you live to be two hundred—and nobody never found gold. You can keep on digging for the whole eternity the good Lord invented, but you'll never find any gold!"

The child heard the big feet moving up on the balcony, then a door shut. He breathed more easily now. He stood up. His fingers began to search the ground again. It was in this exact spot, under the bottom step, that he'd buried the billfold. He dug and dug and his fingers finally touched something that was neither a stone nor hardened earth—leather perhaps? His fingers combed the earth. Stretched out, stiff, the Notary was smiling as though nothing had happened. He spoke, but the black lips in his smiling face did not move. The child wasn't afraid. Spirals of red vapour came from the mouth, like letters unfolding and wrapping themselves around the child.

"There's something more precious than gold and that's love. Love doesn't live in the ground, it lives in the souls of men. A man who loves doesn't need to search for gold."

The Notary smiled but his black mouth was motionless in his grey face. His arm moved and a purple plaster hand held out to the child the billfold he had buried. Fear pounced on the child and striated his body with its claws.

"What's going on, Monsieur Bourdage?"

The Aubergiste had turned on the lights; he was standing in the doorway, staring.

"I never heard nobody yell that loud and I've seen a few things here in this Auberge."

J. J. Bourdage sat up on the edge of his bed, rubbed his eyes and coughed.

"Change this goddamn mattress for me. Gives me nightmares."

Night had come. Soon he would slip into the night like a snake in the rustling grass. He patted his face at the mirror. His beard had grown: every time he carried out a deal his beard grew more heavily. He covered it with lather and shaved. Then he put his suitcase and briefcase on the bed. He put on a clean shirt. He put on his broad-brimmed white hat. Humming, he took the cheques from his briefcase and transferred them to his suitcase. Then, carrying the briefcase, he went downstairs.

"Boss," said J. J. Bourdage to the Aubergiste, giving him the briefcase, "stick that in your safe. It's got the contracts and cheques inside. Gotta take care of them."

The farmers had forgotten cows, calves, pigs. In a cloud of smoke denser than the night they sang and laughed and yelled and the bottles danced and whirled. Three men got up when they saw the white hat; when J. J. Bourdage saw them moving through the cloud of smoke, through the tables, he guessed that they were as drunk as the others. One of them stood before J. J. Bourdage, fists on his haunches.

"It ain't fair. Some people got the right to find gold and others ain't."

"How come your goddamn Company turns up its nose at our land? If the neighbours got gold on their land I don't see why I ain't got no gold on mine."

J. J. Bourdage considered the three men before him. His mind was not yet free of the nightmare.

"Boss! A beer for these men, on the Company! Bring your bottles and come upstairs and see me, in the room I'm using for an office while I'm waiting for the Company to buy the hotel."

J. J. Bourdage rushed up to the room strewn with clothing, objects and maps of the area. The three men arrived, bottle in one hand, billfold in the other.

"We want the Company to dig on our land too!"

J. J. Bourdage unrolled his maps.

"What's the number of your lots?"

The men supplied the details.

"We'll give you our cheques right away."

The cheques fell onto the maps.

"The Company don't take your cheques just to make you happy. Your land's on the Famine River.

"It don't matter to us if they're on the Famine or not."

"If there's a vein of gold in the ground that little river ain't gonna stop it. There ain't enough water in that to satisfy a thirsty calf."

"We just want the same justice as everybody else, the same chance!"

"We want you to look for gold on our land too."

"Take our cheques; you think they smell bad?"

Someone knocked at the door.

"Bring us your contracts, we'll sign the damn things with our eyes shut. We ain't whiners. We can sign a contract without reading it."

"The Company don't want to screw you. I can't take your cheques just to make you happy. Look at the map. You can see the circle. That's where the gold oughtta be, according to our analyses. Your land's outside the circle."

"So when you were here last fall you weren't looking for no moose, you were looking for gold."

The door shook; someone was trying to kick it down.

"Inside the circle or outside the circle, our land can have gold on it as much as anybody else's."

The door opened and it seemed as though the wall were about to come down. Other farmers arrived, waving their cheques. The sight of so much money pouring in should have been a pleasant one, but it was a castastrophe! He had planned and carefully constructed this machine for collecting money, spent a long time smoothing all the gears. It had the dexterity of a pickpocket. But there was one flaw: he couldn't stop it! That troubled him. He had foreseen solutions in case of a breakdown, but so much perfection was disarming. The machine was a too perfect marvel. He had to get away before he was caught in the trap.

"I got to stop collecting your investments. The banks are shut. The Stock Market's shut. We're carrying out illegal operations and the Company's going to turn them down. I can't go against the laws of the Company."

With outstretched arms he began to push the farmers out of his room. When the door was closed he'd go out through the window and down the fire-escape.

"If your Company's a real company you know damn well what it does with the government's laws."

"Tomorrow I'll start the transactions again. Anybody that's left a cheque here gets priority tomorrow."

More cheques fell on the bed.

"The Company don't want to screw you. You don't find gold everywhere."

Driven back, the farmers muttered protests, threats and propositions. Finally they went away, leaving behind them cheques and the smell of cows and tobacco. J. J. Bourdage picked up the money and opened the window. The fire escape shone in the moonlight. A few feet from the bottom step his white Cadillac was waiting for him. He picked up his scattered clothing, grabbed his suitcase, straddled the window-sill. No. It was wrong. He mustn't leave like a thief! He shut the window, opened his suitcase, scattered a few articles of clothing around the room. He'd go down to the first floor, into the roaring celebration. Like someone collecting his strength before he throws himself into cold water, J. J. Bourdage, under his white hat, considered the scene. Joseph-with-the-hand-cut-off, who was standing near him shouted:

"Come to the burial, Monsieur! We're burying our poverty!"

Women and girls had joined the men and through the smoke J. J. Bourdage saw their heads turn towards him. To Joseph-with-the-hand-cut-off:

"The Company didn't promise you it'd find gold. It just promised to look."

The eyes of the man beside him sparkled.

"I wasn't born before the flood. I know about Companies. When they say they're gonna start looking for something it means they already found it!"

"Excuse me," said J. J. Bourdage.

He went over to the Aubergiste and spoke in his ear.

"As of now, the Company won't pay for any more drinks. I don't want nobody to accuse it of trying to drown the local people's faculty to force them to sign."

"If you come on too honest, people won't trust you."

"Your Auberge still isn't for sale?"

"No."

"Don't matter, I'm still buying it."

J. J. Bourdage thought he heard his own name through the din of laughter and bets. He looked up. Someone was saying his name. Over the loudspeaker. He could see hair and a beard on the stage behind the microphone. And the mass of hair had a pair of legs. The people he knew usually had short hair, shaved necks. He was being reprimanded.

"Bourdage! Listen to me. You're an agent of American imperalism. You've come here to buy up our heritage, one lot at a time, and you're going to turn it over to the sharks of multinational capitalism. Bourdage, you're a traitor to the Québécois nation. You've got a soft life for yourself as a result of your alienation and you're making money out of our collective alienation."

"Is that the new singer at the Auberge?" asked a woman who was ready to dart out onto the dance floor.

Her husband held her back.

"Dunno, but you can't dance close to that music."

"Ah, these modern songs! No tune and you can't even understand the words."

"Bourdage," the mass of hair went on, "when our exploited workers start getting diseases from working in the mines, you'll use the profit you've squeezed out of the sweat of their brows, the fortune you've made by mortgaging their lungs, and you'll travel with whores to lands of sea and sun."

The Aubergiste cut off the power to the microphone and put on a record. The loudspeakers bleated out a love song. No one was listening to the song from the mass of hair with flabby little arms and legs sticking out of it.

This outlandish character had given J. J. Bourdage a sign that he should be on his way—and fast.

"Don't stop you from smiling, does it?" asked the Aubergiste.

"Boss, in this life if somebody can't take an insult he's better off hiding under his mother's skirt."

He could feel the weight of his Big Deal straining his muscles. His back couldn't be any more tired if he'd carried all the rocks off all the land in this village. And the thirst! But he mustn't drink. Smoke? Light up a cigar to surround himself with his own smoke? The farmers would stop trusting him if he wasn't smoking a cigar. Sit down. He walked into the cloud of the celebration. A chair appeared before him. Faces approached him, shining with light reflected off the bottles they brought to their lips.

"You think we got a chance of getting rich?"

Here in this out-of-the-way village, on this night which he was forbidden to flee, he must once again invent, lie, gamble, improvise.

"You want me to tell you if you're gonna get rich? That I can't say. I know it's what you want to hear, but the Company don't want to screw you. One thing I can tell you, though: it's never been the Company's policy to hang out with poor people. Because poverty's a germ, you know, and it's catching. But so's getting rich!"

An old man with a bald pointed head, toothless, tried to catch J. J. Bourdage's attention.

"At my age! At my age! Young people can spend their money by the shovelful, but all I'm gonna be able to do is be buried in my own gold!"

The shoemaker put his arm around J. J. Bourdage's shoulder:

"You know, Monsieur Bourdage, last fall you were the laughing-stock of the village. You tried to make us think you were a moose-hunter and we believed you. Only thing was, we laughed till our teeth fell out when we saw you hunting for moose with your nose stuck to the ground as if a moose was some little animal the size of a blueberry! Holy Virgin, we laughed! But how about you? Did you ever see any gold veins with your naked eye?"

"Some of the people around here," said Arrache-Clou, "they went right to the end of their land, over by the Famine River. Of course their eyes were naked and them, they didn't see nothing.

"When I think that we thought you were looking for moose under the blueberry bushes!"

Around him there were no more faces, only open mouths overflowing with laughter and the smell of tobacco dissolving in the smell of beer.

"The most important quality for a gold-hunter," said Bourdage, "is discretion. I couldn't dress myself up like a moose, so I dressed up like a hunter instead."

"If you know there's gold under all the rocks on our land, can you guess how many gold teeth I got in my mouth?"

J. J. Bourdage couldn't refuse the challenge. All the mouths around him were closed. There were only eyes now, staring at him, ears that were waiting. J. J. Bourdage examined the man, whose thick hair fell into his eyes.

"Tell me! If you know what you're talking about. A tooth in a mouth ain't as deep as a gold mine under the ground."

"I never said exactly how much gold there was on your land, but one thing I know for sure. You paid too much for those gold teeth. Dentist's gold. You got screwed!"

The man with the thick hair falling into his eyes got up, knocking over his chair, and went out. He jumped into his car and everyone was sure he was heading for Saint-Georges-de-Beauce to get a refund from his dentist. Laughing mouths reappeared in the smoke.

"Me," said Oliva Beauchamp, "my father always suspected there was something on this land. He often used to show me shiny streaks in the rocks. And my late father, he'd say: 'I got a pretty good idea that's gold.' He'd put them rocks in a separate pile and he'd be real careful not to break them. My father, he never thought of talking about it to nobody except his kids. Not even his wife. He was scared people'd think he was crazy."

"Yes," J. J. Bourdage confirmed, "you gotta be crazy to

hunt for gold."

"Well, that's a hell of a good piece of news!" exclaimed a bald man with hair in his ears. "I'm fed up with being a quiet ox harnessed to my goddamn land that don't want to follow me. It'd be a hell of a good thing to be crazy. Crazy as a loon! Crazy enough to be locked up!"

"It wouldn't take a very big chunk of gold to drive me crazy!"

"A slice of bread and butter with gold on it in the morning, another one at noon and another one at night! A man'd get fed up."

"How many years is it we've been eating our bread and butter with misery–morning noon and night?"

"We're fed up too!"

"If we were really fed up we wouldn't be here!"

"But if we weren't here we wouldn't have no gold!"

On stage, the musicians were struggling to bombard the land with music; they threw out sound with the energy of someone throwing pebbles at the stars. Around J. J. Bourdage all the mouths were talking at once. He is alone. He loves no one. No one loves him. He wants to leave, it's urgent, he must slip away; but on the other side of the night, at the end of his road, he will be just as alone as he is here in this Auberge, which has become an enormous drum that musicians in a trance are beating at the same rhythm as their pounding hearts. A mouth spits moist words into his ear:

"You don't have to worry about gold; you swim in it all day long, just like the rest of us are wading around in mud and manure."

J. J. Bourdage felt an urge to tell him the truth, as others sometimes feel an urge to lie. But the truth is forbidden to him. On the road he has chosen, truth does not exist. Nor falsehood. All that exists is the next step to be taken. All that exists is the uncertain earth of the vast night where he must put down his foot for the next step.

"Gold?" he asked. "Seems to me the more you're holding the bigger our hands grow!"

How did he manage to laugh heartily as he said that? He spread his fingers and exhibited them all around, flapping them like the wings of a bird.

"Hey! It's true! He's got hands the size of shovels!"

"Gold! I pray the good Lord'll show you as much as I've seen!"

He'd taken the step. He'd put down his foot. Lying gave him a pleasure that still surprised him. When would he be able to leave? All these faces together, the mouths, the laughter, the eyes reflecting the gold that shone in their dreams, the dancing bottles, the brown hands with fingers that looked like roots, all these people formed a wall that was thicker than the wall of his cell. He could only lie again.

"One thing that's more precious than gold is believing you can find some. What's underneath the floor?"

"There's five hundred cases of beer in the cellar."

"And what's underneath those cases?"

"The cement floor."

"And what's underneath the cement floor?"

"Bedrock."

"And under the bedrock?"

In a single voice all the mouths proclaimed:

"GOLD!"

"And still," J. J. Bourdage went on, "this is some of the poorest land in the country."

"I think you're right: around here hay grows like wool on a cow's back."

"That's generally the first indication that there's gold."

Saying these words he raised an index finger with a large ring sparkling on it.

"Gold," said Oliva Beauchamp, "must pull all the wealth on the land down with it."

J. J. Bourdage pointed to his index finger with its golden ring.

"There's one thing in this world that's worth more than gold. And I can tell you that because the Company won't. The thing that's worth more than gold is love. Love's something I've held in my hands more often than gold. If the good Lord invented love that's the proof that he's more than perfect."

Why did J.J. Bourdage have tears in his eyes? No one dared to ask him. The eyes around him didn't know where to look. Everyone was silent. All the bottles leaped to the mouths at once.

"Give us some gold, then we'll go hunting for love!"

The laughter fell onto him with the force of a powerful wave.

"When the time comes to lie down in the ground, even if a man's coffin's full of gold, he's gotta be pretty sad if he dies without love. A man that dies without love, he's like a ghost, a sad ghost, that's gonna roam around like a lost soul. That's what the Notary, a man from around here, said."

The people around him saw his lips move but the ear-splitting song from the orchestra erased the words in his mouth. In the back, in shadows caressed by shafts of coloured light, the dancers moved with exquisite care, as though they were dancing on gold. J. J. Bourdage, a tired swimmer who sees the shoreline too far in the distance, repeated to himself that he mustn't let himself be swallowed up. Go on. Declare that you have to go on. Make every effort not to give up. Persist. Don't run away. Wait. Soon he'd be able to dart into the night. He pushed back his big white hat.

"Want to dance?" asked a woman who had her bosom on the table and her arms around her neighbours' shoulders.

"No thanks. I gotta be going."

"Whoa there, don't go too far away. We'll come and get you!"

"I'm going to bed, all by myself like a holy man. Gold's a very jealous mistress."

"Wow! You hear that, you men? Monsieur Bourdage is going to fornicate with his gold! Ha ha!"

You could no longer hear the orchestra which was struggling without a voice. The singer was mute. The guitars had stopped cooing. The silence pierced your ears. The Aubergiste fiddled under the television set that hung from the ceiling.

"They're talking about gold! They're talking about gold! They're talking about us!"

He turned off the orchestra's electricity. He yelled so loud that everyone finally turned around to look at the television set.

"They're talking about gold! They're talking about us!"

J. J. Bourdage crumpled; the exhausted swimmer let himself drift. All around him people applauded and hopped and poured beer; mouths swallowed and drank; eyes wept. The Aubergiste plugged the orchestra in again and it exploded with joy. Delirium burst in the arteries. He was silent.

"They said we found gold!"

"We found gold!"

Feeling his chair sway, J. J. Bourdage thought: "It's a heart attack!" Hopelessly, he rubbed his chest. As he opened his eyes he realized that hands had picked up his chair, that he was being lifted up at arms' length—in triumph! His only desire was to flee, but he had been annointed emperor. He was God above his clouds. And inside they were screaming, applauding, giving him an ovation. The guitars whined and the drummers pounded as though they were accompanying an earthquake. Everywhere beneath him he saw bottles of beer, and their blinking reflections.

"Gold! Gold!"

Ephrem Poulin, a farmer from the fifth concession, had signed a cheque ceding to the Company the right to prospect his land. His brother Euchariste Poulin, an elevator operator by profession, had the right to inspect the paternal farm, by virtue of their late father's will. So Ephrem had called Euchariste in Montreal to tell him about his investment. In his elevator, Euchariste Poulin was bored. To pass the time he wore, attached to his belt, a transistor radio of which he wasn't very proud, because it was an old one. An old Japanese one. All day long he listened to station CJMS, the toe-tapping music station. Very often CJMS invited its "thousands of listeners" to call in and tell what they'd seen: "News for all by all!" For each piece of news read on the air, CJMS generously offered a prize: a new transistor. Euchariste would be very happy to witness a holdup, a murder, a rape or an accident. But he'd been condemned all his life to hew wood and draw water on a rocky land; he'd never been entitled to do anything else. And he was tired of the ham sandwiches with mustard he'd been condemned to eat for years. The only carnage he might ever witness would be the crash of his own elevator, and he wouldn't even be there to phone in the news to CJMS. And so when Ephrem called to tell him they were hunting for gold on the paternal farm he assumed it had already been found. Before asking for his legal share, he realized that along with gold comes luck; he called CJMS and told them gold had been found. The news was read into the CJMS microphone. A reporter from Télé-Métropole heard it and immediately reported that gold had been found in a poor region of Quebec. When a Radio-Canada reporter responsible for covering special events heard of this extraordinary discovery, he felt as though the wind had been knocked out of him. How had Radio-Canada with its 27,000 employees, managed to miss this scoop? When he got his breath back he ran to a studio, grabbed a microphone and announced that "according to specialists, we can now say that there is gold in Bellechasse County and oil in Arabia!" Another reporter, bald and corpulent, who let his beard grow to try to conceal these two signs of approaching age, had managed, after many efforts, to persuade a young working girl who was hitchhiking to get into his car. The radio was playing Mantovani. Then the music was interrupted by a special news bulletin. He was only half listening, busily smiling at the girl. Bellechasse, gold, Arabia: the words suddenly came together. His smile was erased. He stepped on the accelerator. The car sprang forward. People looked at him with admiration. The bald corpulent reporter sped to the nearest restaurant where he telephoned the news room that "informed sources confirm that the Arabs will probably invest in the development of gold mines in Bellechasse County, Quebec." Because of the international importance of this news and taking into account the possible economic repercussions, the sports news was interrupted and the announcer read: "The Arabs have approached Quebec with a bilateral agreement pertaining to gold and oil: oil for gold or gold for oil? This is the two-pronged question being asked. The answer will not come from the federal capital or the provincial capital. It might be found in Washington." And so the villagers learned that there was more than pebbles and rocks in their land.

When J. J. Bourdage heard the delirium on the television, he wanted to get up and run to his white Cadillac, without his suitcase or cheques. But he had been lifted into the air by the joyous people: a celebrated god, he was even tempted to believe what he'd heard on television.

The Aubergiste put bottles on the tables and brought J. J. Bourdage the bottle of champagne a pair of newlyweds had left in their room, probably because they were afraid of intoxication on their wedding night. J. J. Bourdage popped the cork and sprinkled the heads of his bearers.

"That's what it's like to be rich! Don't take any more than that to be rich!"

The ceiling was too low. The room was too narrow. Everyone was on their feet, dancing madly as music, beer and sweat flowed like water. If the celebration continued, the walls would come down. He had to duck his head to keep from hitting the ceiling. His chair leaped from arm to arm, hands reached out to touch him—men's hands, women's hands. The women had the most curious hands in the province! The houses in the village emptied. People raced to the Auberge du Bon Boire, making their way through hysterical cars. Petit-Lecourt, tied up in front of his house with his dog, Arthur's, chain, saw the village stirred up, saw shadows and cars crossing on the main street as though it were a wedding night. He interrogated the starry sky.

"Husband?" his wife called.

He ran to her, dragging his chain.

"Arthur needs his chain."

She unfastened the knot at her husband's belt and attached the chain to Arthur's collar.

"They found gold on our land. I heard it on the TV."

"See, I was right to go looking."

"If it's true, stop wasting time; go get your shovel and dig!"

The new arrivals hesitated at the door of the Auberge, dumbfounded, but they were caught up in the tumult and soon they were dancing and bellowing in triumph.

"Gold! Gold! Gold! Gold! Gold! Gold!"

The very vault of the sky trembled with the echoes. Here and there men were weeping: they had spent their whole lives struggling against stubborn stones and now they couldn't enter this dream. The women were jubilant. One fat woman said: "It's too much, it's too much! I've got to do something!" She climbed up on the table and got undressed, tossing her garments at anyone at all. Another woman seized a man by the arm and took him off to the grass on the hill, on the other side of the Auberge parking lot. In the corner was an old woman too rheumatic to dance and with a voice too thin to shout with the others. She said her rosary so that God would rebuild the church before she died! The Widow Gros-Douillette danced, her widow's bosom heaving to the four horizons: "With all this gold we're going to find husbands!" The Aubergiste stood up on his counter, asked for silence and yelled:

"There's a man from Sainte-Germaine that wants to talk."

The man climbed up on the counter and shouted into a megaphone.

"My name's Siméon Gousse and I sell Buicks and Chryslers. If you're walking on gold you oughtta be driving one of my cars! The cars are outside, in front of the hotel. If you want them, take them. You can pay tomorrow, gold on the barrel!"

Everyone shot towards the door. Only a few were able to make their way through the kicking and punching. With bloody noses and black eyes they took possession of the new cars and set off, their wheels digging into the ground. The others returned, sad. Fascinated by the dream they hadn't been able to realize, silent, they sat at tables overflowing with bottles. The woman who had got undressed looked for her clothes. No one pinched her behind. Foam remained on the necks of bottles. J. J. Bourdage had experienced motionless time in the scribbled-on walls of his cell, but this night time passed even more slowly. He wished he could find a concealed door. Bébert Lapierre spotted the cap belonging to Antoine Bouton, the taxi-driver.

"Antoine Bouton, take me to the Château Frontenac in Quebec City!"

The Château Frontenac is a big hotel where rich men sleep at least once before they die.

"How about your wife, Bébert?" asked Antoine Bouton.

"We're rich now so we act like the rich. Everybody lives his own life!"

Everyone respected the Postman's Widow. If she didn't like you she could keep your letters in a drawer. People moved aside for her, cars slowed down, lovers' shoulders moved apart and the bouquet she carried wasn't even grazed in the general scuffle. When she came up to J. J. Bourdage she pulled out the African violets and stuck the flowerpot in his hands.

"Monsieur, is there gold in this earth?"

To avoid being impolite he refrained from telling her she was out of her mind, but stuck his fingers in the rich moist soil. He touched something hard. A pebble? He pulled out the object: a wad of bills rolled up in a plastic bag.

"Of course there's gold in your earth, Madame!"

The miracle left everyone breathless. They applauded as Jesus must have been applauded at the marriage at Cana when he changed water into wine.

No one knew that the Postman's Widow had the habit of putting her small savings into the earth in her flowerpots for safekeeping. Even she had forgotten. Not a single woman was left now in the Auberge du Bon Boire. All had run to dig in their flowerpots. Gradually the men followed them, pretending they were in no hurry and not curious.

A man approached J. J. Bourdage, holding a piece of yellow paper.

"Hello, Monsieur le Maire!"

"You remember me, Monsieur Bourdage?"

"Last fall when I told you about my plan for a Big Deal you encouraged me. Monsieur le Maire, gratitude's something not even an iron file could erase from my memory!"

"I want to tell you officially, in the name of our fellow citizens that we represent and whose best interests we defend, I want to tell you—now where'd I put that piece of paper? Ah, here it is—that gold in this village is going to be real good for wealth and real bad for poverty. In my own personal name I'd like to add a little joke my wife thought was pretty funny: now we got all this gold, let's hope nobody gets the fever!"

He held out a telegram.

"This is from our M.P."

J. J. Bourdage read the message.

"I answered that he oughtta be sending a telegram to congratulate you, not me."

"Monsieur le Maire, I think so much of you that if there's no gold on your land the Company's going to have some put there!"

He picked up a bottle of beer and offered it to the Mayor, who sat respectfully close to J. J. Bourdage, bowing diffidently in the presence of the great capitalist. Not a single plant in the village still had its roots in the earth in its pot. The women returned, disappointed and a little sad beneath the laughing masks of makeup they had just reapplied.

"The earth in my flowerpot comes from my land. There wasn't any gold in it," moaned a woman who didn't dare to approach J. J. Bourdage.

He was responsible for every jolt in the life beneath the large black cover of this village; he was the source of all joy and all disappointment. All he wanted was a few cheques. All he wanted was to be able to get away and look like an honest man. And then change his name again. Change his hair style. Change his face. Try to lead an ordinary life. And let himself once again drift away on the current of his mad dreams.

The men had come back too. Like a sudden blaze, the dance! The men and women twisted and twitched and fluttered and scuttled. The night, filled with emotion, was becoming intoxicated with a marvellous new day. Only J. J. Bourdage was unhappy. His Big Deal was not obeying his meticulously set-out plans. Women's arms were quarrelling over him. He murmured to them, his lips in their hair.

"Gotta bury the past. Live for today. Your life's gonna change, Madame."

"Maybe it is, Monsieur Bourdage, but my old man ain't gonna turn to gold. He's gonna be what he's always been—a piece of . . ."

Men's hands patted his back, men's arms squeezed his shoulders. He hated being liked. It irritated him.

"They lick my feet but when I take off with their blessed money they'll be throwing rocks at me!"

The villagers were celebrating their own birth. The orchestra spat out fiery sounds. The dancers shook like rubble in a gold-digger's sieve. The Aubergiste was able to weave over to J. J. Bourdage.

"The phone!"

Salvation! Escape. He would explain that he had to go to New York to see the President of the Company.

"Hello!"

"Monsieur J. J. Bourdage. One moment please, the Minister wants to talk to you."

"The Minister?"

"Here's the Honourable Minister of Justice for Quebec."

"Justice?"

There was no one left in the Auberge, no dancing or music; the walls had come together, leaving only the walls of a cell.

"Hello Monsieur Bourdage."

"Yes, Monsieur the Honourable Minister. Speaking."

"The Quebec Minister of Justice would like to congratulate you personally on your success. Through my information department, Monsieur Bourdage, I've learned how many obstacles you overcame to attain success. I congratulate you for your tenacity, personally. Monsieur Bourdage, don't be offended, but I'd say that altar boys might find cruets of wine and incense but no altar boy's going to find gold! Ha ha!"

The laughter of the Minister, surprised to find his joke so funny, risked cracking the telephone receiver.

"Monsieur Bourdage, now I'd like to speak to you officially, not as a friend but as the Minister of Justice of

Quebec. Roads strewn with obstacles are the hardest roads, the muddiest, the dustiest; they dirty your hands; you understand me?"

"Yes, Monsieur le Ministre."

"If you ever need to wash your hand—you understand?—rest assured that as Minister of Justice for Quebec, as a personal friend and as a shareholder in your company I'll be glad to help you."

"Shareholder in my company?"

"Monsieur Bourdage, as a sign of good faith I'd like to suggest that as of tonight I buy a few hundred dollars worth of shares in your company. My accountant will speak to you tomorrow about a larger investment. List the purchase in my wife's name. Her maiden name."

J. J. Bourdage was barely breathing, as though the telephone cord were wrapped around his neck.

"Monsieur le Ministre, when a man does me a favour, even if I don't meet him till Judgement Day, I'll recognize that man, even if he's all chewed up. And I'll tell him thanks, thanks for helping me get clean."

"Monsieur Bourdage, one of our mutual friends who practises the strange, the very strange trade of prison Governor, recommended you to me very warmly. As you know, he's just built an exquisite new house. He wouldn't hesitate to mortgage it to buy some shares in your company."

"Don't let him mortgage anything! I owe him a lot. When a man does me a favour I don't forget it."

"Monsieur Bourdage, I congratulate you. It's people like you that prove we aren't working in vain. And I'd ask you to congratulate all your friends as well. They've got hearts of gold! Ha ha!"

"Monsieur le Ministre, would you grant me a privilege? Would you agree to say hello to my friends?"

"Yes, Monsieur Bourdage, I will take great pleasure in granting them the honour of speaking to those gallant folks."

With the force of a drill-shaft going through bedrock, J. J. Bourdage cleared a passage through the dancers, who clung to one another as closely as gold hugged the rock, and snatched the microphone from the singer.

"Mesdames, Messieurs, silence. The Government's on the phone."

He went back to the telephone holding the microphone,

going through the villagers who didn't want to stop dancing now, through couples who didn't want to separate, pushing, elbowing, kicking. Some clinging couples were still dancing, deaf to the silence of the orchestra, stunned by the music of their own joy.

"Are you there, Monsieur le Maire? Monsieur le Maire?"

When he heard his name the Mayor started, removing his hand too nervously from Madame Petit-Lecourt's brassiere. So nervously in fact that he broke the strap. The proud edifice crumbled. The Mayor's hand had already flown to the telephone.

"Monsieur le Ministre, this is the Mayor of the village; he'll repeat your message."

"Hello, Monsieur le Maire," said the Minister.

"Hello, Monsieur le Maire," repeated the Mayor, faithfully following his instructions.

His voice, amplified by the loudspeakers, spread over the couples. They made no distinction between the Mayor's spluttering voice and the music imported from an enchanted island by an intoxicated bird that had whispered it in the ear of musicians even more intoxicated, who now were playing it for drunken dancers.

"It is a great honour for me to congratulate . . ."

"It is a great honour for me to tabulate . . ."

"And congratulate your Mayor . . ."

"And tabulate the chairs . . ."

". . . as well as Monsieur Bourdage without whom you would never have known that your land is worth gold . . ."

". . . as well as Monsieur Bourdage who's worth his weight in gold!"

A small warm hand grabbed J. J. Bourdage's arm. It was the Curé. Behind him stood a pretty girl he'd glimpsed once before at the presbytery.

"It's your altar boy!" he couldn't resist saying, with a wink at the girl.

The Curé's face turned so brilliantly red that J. J. Bourdage realized he'd made a mistake.

"Excuse me," he said, trying to be diplomatic. "Monsieur le Curé, I know there's people that prefer little boys, but it's more natural for a man to like women, eh? A man without a woman's a sad man, eh?"

How could a man unfamiliar with the village gossip pierce with a single look the Curé's conscience and uncover the secret buried there? With such penetrating eyes it wasn't surprising he'd found gold on this miserable land.

"I hope," said the Curé, "that you give thanks to God for the gift that allows you to know the deepest secrets. And I hope you'll use it for your celestial salvation."

"As Monsieur le Curé showed in his last sermon," said Miss Catechism, "God's gifts are gold nuggets that he lends to man for his terrestrial voyage; and man must give him an accounting when he returns to the Paternal house."

"Gold," concluded the Curé, "is a mirror that must reflect the face of God."

J. J. Bourdage tapped him on the shoulder.

"Don't worry, Monsieur le Curé, the first thing we're going to do with the good Lord's gold is we're gonna build him a foundation for his church. Yes Monsieur le Curé, a golden foundation if that's what you want!"

The Curé fell to his knees and Miss Catechism squeezed against him, devoutly taking his hand.

"Oh my Lord, my Lord, my Lord!"

The Curé was silent. No words came from his mouth. Only tears, silent words, burst from his eyes. His arms outstretched, the Curé whispered:

"My Lord! My Lord! Why do you accord such joy to your son who offends you every day . . ."

Miss Catechism dropped the Curé's hand.

". . . and sometimes even twice a day . . ."

Miss Catechism picked up the Curé's hand again.

"Sometimes even three times!" she accused herself.

The young woman's sobs shook her lovely bosom. If J. J. Bourdage could confess to her he would lay his penitent head against her beautiful and forgiving bosom. He didn't want to think of the warmth where he could lay his head. He mustn't sink into desire. Lie and flee. He wanted nothing but the intoxication of sitting in a white Cadillac, holding the steering wheel, stepping on the accelerator along bumpy roads, hunched over the wheel, his head grazing the sky. He wanted to close his eyes and not see the sky or the earth on this night that he must cross until the light of day and then open them to lie down in a room like a stylish cell.

"The good Lord sent you to our little village."

"Let's say it was the Company. But the good Lord's likely got a few shares."

The priest and the young woman bowed their heads and

folded their hands. J. J. Bourdage heard himself say:

"Monsieur le Curé, I've committed every sin in the book."

Lie, tell the truth, there was no difference, everything was a lie.

"My son, man is made of earth. And what's more monstrous than the earth? It's dirty, it's muddy. We find—and this is quite normal—mud in the soul of man. Man is made of earth. And don't we find in the earth disgusting creatures as slimy as sin? Earthworms, centipedes, larvae, all those animals with no eyes, all those animals that crawl and make you sick to your stomach? Man is made of earth and all those ignoble animals crawl inside him. It's God's will. But it's also God's will that hidden in the mud among the slimy crawling animals of his creatures made of earth, there should be gold. Yes, my son, despite your faults, you must know that there are veins of gold in you that run through your corruption like the veins in your body."

J. J. Bourdage wanted to laugh, laugh like the others, uproariously, but he didn't have the right.

"My son, I'm going to ask God to bless your undertaking."

The Curé raised his arms to Heaven and you could hear, louder than the music turned feverish by gold, the flapping of vast wings.

"The Holy Ghost!" thought J. J. Bourdage.

"A helicopter! A beautiful helicopter! With little lights!"

The dancing stopped. Pale little men got out of the machine and darted around the room with tangled wires, spotlights rudely aimed at faces, and cameras that poked their noses everywhere. The pale little men, who smelled like women, asked:

"Are you glad that gold's been found in your underdeveloped country?"

The pale little men held out their microphones as though they were weapons. The villagers moved their noses away, their words cut off on the tips of their tongues. The microphone was under Rosette Sarrazin's nose; she wanted to talk but she'd forgotten the question. Behind her, Tristesse Lachance said:

"Sure, we're real glad."

The camera tried to pick up the man who had spoken.

The large eye spotted him.

"But we had gold already," Tristesse Lachance went on. "You know the song:

They're golden they're golden
They're priceless treasures
They're golden they're golden . . ."

"Tell us, my fine fellow, tell our vast audience, just what is it that's golden?"

"The Curé's little dog's turds!"

Laughter lifted the ceiling. The old woman sitting alone at a table in the corner drank her beer. She thought, God probably hasn't often heard laughter like that coming off his sad earth. When she was in Heaven would she hear the laughter of the people in her village? Her soul rose at this question, but her body was still too heavy. If she found gold in her garden she'd take it to Paradise and then let it drift like snow over the land of those whose laughter God had never heard.

"And you, young man," asked the pale little man with the microphone, "what do you think now that you don't have to work for a living?"

A few whose eyes weren't closed by drunkenness recognized, in the halo of the spotlights, the hairy bearded young man who had insulted J. J. Bourdage earlier that evening.

"Officially it's the exploitation of the turkeys. And you media guys live off the culture of the turkeys. Gold's an imposture. There was once a great poet called Balzac, and once he heard there was gold in some city in Italy. So he got in his buggy and went off to Italy. When people hear the word 'gold' everybody turns into a turkey, even great geniuses. There was a great modern painter named Hernious Bosch that painted people so rich they were eating gold. And do you know what those rich people do? They shit gold. Yes, Monsieur. And that ain't good for your health."

The pale little man with the microphone turned his head towards the pale little man who was sweating behind the camera.

"These goddamn peasants are still in their anal period."

"We're not alone!" said the other one, squeaking like a mouse whose tail is being bitten.

"Well Grandpa, now they've found gold around here, what's your reaction?"

He was a shrivelled old man, waving a carved cane. Instead of leaning on it he carried it over his shoulder, like an axe or a rifle.

"I'll tell you, young man, if they've found gold today it's because our fathers and grandfathers and our ancestors—and our grandmothers too—they hollered and screamed for generations. Our parents lived off the land for a long long time, like dogs gnawing on a bone that's as dry as a rock. That gold they found today, it's our fathers' tears!"

"Will it transform your life?"

"I been around longer than you, young man, and I just hope the gold ain't gonna change back into tears."

"And how about you, Monsieur, what do you think of the gold?"

"It gives off a hell of a shine! You know, we won't need street-lights at night any more. We'll just take away a little dirt and the gold underneath it's gonna shine in the moonlight. I guess we'll have to take our shovels in the morning and throw a little dirt over the gold. Yup, it'll be hard work. But we'll be able to afford niggers to do it for us."

"Madame! Madame!"

A fat woman, Rosette Sarrazin, had fallen asleep with her head on her neighbour's shoulder. She opened her eyes, stung by the spotlights.

"Tell us what you think of the gold."

"Ever since Jesus was born, every year the Three Wise Men take a few more steps across the earth. Tonight they made it to our village. Thank you, Three Wise Men. If you need a place for your camels, come to our place. But there ain't no baby Jesus in my stable."

"Hey!" announced one of the pale little men. "Here's one that's still sober. Say, Monsieur, tell us what the gold represents for you."

"Well, here's what I think. The rich are always waiting to get poor. And the poor are always waiting to get rich. We're waiting. The whole world's waiting."

"You don't have to wait now, you've found gold."

"But now we're scared as hell we'll lose it. Now I'm rich I don't feel any happier than when I was poor. You know, poor people shouldn't complain. When I was poor I didn't have a care in the world. Frankly, the poor are a lot happier than the rich. But I had to get rich to find that out."

A dry, flinty woman hurled herself into the area lit by the spotlights. It was the Postman's Widow. She raised her head high to show the camera her fine but determined chin.

"You think that individual's the one that discovered the gold today?"

With a disdainful finger she pointed to the white hat of J. J. Bourdage who couldn't bolt beneath the watchful and curious eye of the camera.

"They found gold around here years and years ago," she said with certainty.

From her bag she extirpated a roll of paper which she freed from its ribbon bow.

"This is a confidential paper that the hand of fate entrusted to me when I was doing my work at the Post Office. The author is deceased. Peace to his ashes! Listen to how he described his discovery:

Land of gold

I have found threads of gold
forbidden to the mortals of this earth.
Now dead, I roam beneath the earth,
Following these veins of gold
That lead to you, my treasure."

The Postman's Widow rolled up her paper then, thinking better of it, she unwound it again to reread:

"I found veins of gold
forbidden to the mortals of this earth . . ."

"You hear that? 'Forbidden to mortals?' "

She glared into the camera.

"Messieurs of the Television, Caillouette the Notary who was a great unknown poet because he was too modest, discovered the existence of gold in our land. And everybody that comes after him's a phoney!"

She pointed a threatening finger at the man in the white hat. J. J. Bourdage resisted the pale little men who wanted to put him before the camera.

"Tomorrow. Come back tomorrow. Tonight we celebrate."

"If the Notary found gold when he was alive," threatened the Postman's Widow, "I predict he ain't gonna let his property be stolen!"

The camera and microphone had already jumped to another location, before an old man's toothless mouth.

"Have you been informed, Monsieur, that a Government

Ministry has ordered a soil analysis for your region?"

"Us, you know, we leave politics alone."

"Officials have concluded that the population should be moved to more fertile land. What do you think of that?

"Kiddies, officials sit with their asses on their chairs; but we got gold under ours!"

"And you, Monsieur? You're a peasant, I can smell it. What does gold suggest to you?"

"First of all, you ain't got very good manners. Maybe we're peasants but we can tell the difference between a man and a woman."

"And you, what do you think? If you think . . ."

At the microphone, Chou Racine, a short round man, warm as fresh bread.

"When we were being brought up they taught us more fairy tales than real things. Now I ain't blaming nobody: when you ain't got nothing at least if you invent something you got your own fibs. One time after a rainstorm we saw a rainbow at the back of the field and that rainbow was as pretty as if it was painted on the blue sky with fresh paint. My father, he said to me: 'If I wasn't in such a rush and I didn't have so many cows or pigs or kids or headaches I'd go and hunt for the end of the rainbow because underneath it there's a pot of gold.' So me, I walked across those fields practically as far as the horizon and I climbed up on top of those mountains of rocks and I even got up on top of the spruce trees, heading straight for that rainbow. But I lost sight of it! When I told my father I'd lost the rainbow my father, he said that the rainbow'd likely taken off and gone to another country and I'd got there too late. Believe it or not, when bombs were going through the sound barrier I was still thinking there was gold at the end of the rainbow. The only thing is, you mustn't get there too late. Today, it's just the right time. My father must be laughing out of the other side of his face—if it ain't all rotten by now."

One of the pale little men from the television climbed up on the stage.

"Mesdames et Messieurs, I would ask you to resume your quaint and no doubt highly significant dancing. The orchestra will start playing again. Really put your hearts in your dancing now. Our cameras will record the image of people dancing on gold."

"And while the people are dancing, American companies are buying up our land, one lot at a time," a voice threw in, the voice of the hairy bearded young man who wasn't being listened to.

"Hold hands," ordered the television man, "and don't be ashamed to show the entire world your happiness and pride."

Legs were raised and lowered, bodies pushed to left and right; they jumped and hands joined other hands; fingers crossed, they formed a cordon of arms that twisted, stretched, undulated. The music grew wilder, lost its head. The same blood flowed in the veins of all the villagers, they had a single heart. As they danced they felt as though they were travelling around the earth, that their feet were making it spin like a big ball. Faster and faster! The music was the cry in their mouths.

The joyous villagers and their dazzled wives, who supported one another's drunkenness, wove through the crowds of cars, climbed onto the roofs, jumped from car to car, went in through one door and out the other; they crawled joyously, zigzagging through the night like a vine in the grass; an orchestra played for them from the other side of the night. J. J. Bourdage was a ring on the laughing serpent of festive villagers. The two hands holding his gripped as hard as though they were holding gold nuggets. When it reached the main street–the only one–the serpent headed for the top of the mountain and ran to the church, which seemed to have been devoured by big black teeth. Around the church, throats remembered litanies and feet recalled processions. The round slowed down, then stopped. Joy turned to piety. The silence of the great night above the ashes of the church slipped coldly onto faces and shoulders. Suddenly, cries struck the night like lightning.

"Help! Thief! Help! Murder!"

The Curé remembered–why?–his college days. At the same time he remembered when he had reigned over his church. He remembered the applause in the theatre at his college. And he remembered his sermons, during which no one snoozed–which was not the case for his colleague in the next parish. He dropped Miss Catechism's hand and ran into the ashes, through the crumbled stones, the charred beams, the sharp debris, to the pulpit. The metal staircase was twisted by the flames, but it hadn't been devastated. He climbed it, seeing nothing, as though he were climbing into the night.

"Who's that yelling? Who's that yelling?"

"Turn on the lights!"

Motors roared. Beams from headlights searched the night, through the rubbish. They spotted the Curé and lighted him, standing, high in the night, and his words struck the night as though it were the skin of a drum.

"Heaven, be fair! I'm lost, murdered, my throat has been cut, they've made off with my gold. Who can it be? What's become of him? Where is he? Where is he hiding? What can I do to find him? Where can I run? Or not run? Isn't he there? Isn't he here? Who is it? Stop. Wretch, give me back my gold!"

The villagers had never seen their Curé so painfully distraught. He was in tatters. Not even the night when the church had been destroyed had the weeping Curé shown so much sorrow. A strong hand was placed on J. J. Bourdage's shoulder.

"It wouldn't be you that took his gold?"

A man feeling so much sorrow is entitled to be left alone, not to be overwhelmed with consolation. A man has the right to be left alone with his unhappiness. The dance was over. The villagers' hands dropped to their sides. They moved away. Their cars dispersed. Night fell on the Curé in his pulpit among the ruins. He wanted to hear the enthusiastic applause of abbés and seminarians when the curtain fell. But this night was as silent as though some great disaster had demolished everything. The silence wasn't complete, though. Applause! Two small hands clapping with conviction. Miss Catechism was waiting for him at the foot of the stairs. The Curé questioned the night. Why was the night so vast? It was too vast for a single man. Had God not invented the night to push men towards one another, push them together in the night, lead them to love one another? The Curé touched Miss Catechism's hair.

"I'd rather touch your hair than have all the gold in the village."

The villagers had scattered and invaded the stables. They untied the cows and sent them out with kicks. They broke down the fences around the calves. The astonished animals obeyed, mooing. They opened the bars in the fields and fences fell.

"We're all free—us and the cows and the calves!"

Free, the animals didn't know where to go in the good Lord's night. The bulls didn't come near the cows who wanted only to go back to their warm straw. The animals were confused. They heard only shouting that wasn't part of normal human language. Children and men whom they loved were now handling them roughly, moving crazily and laughing in a way that didn't cover the silence of the night.

"Now we got gold we don't need your milk! Scram!"

As the animals were struck they moaned, not understanding; they ran and turned around in circles, looking for their stables, looking for the sun.

"When I think," said a woman, "I'll never have to bend down under those animals again and pull their tits . . ."

"Whew!"

How could the animals suspect what hope and sorrow was contained in these words? They lowed, waiting to find out where they would sleep. At times they would be kicked in the sides and at times they would be stroked on the muzzle. Why the blows? Why the caresses? Every man, every woman, every child pursued his animal. They ran as far as they could, pushing down barriers, taking down fences; when they were sure they'd taken their animal so far it couldn't find the way back to the stable the men, women and children returned.

They turned their backs on the animals and saw flames. They ran. The stables were on fire.

"We're through with stables and cows and manure; now's the time for gold!" said a villager who stood with folded arms, looking on with a smile of tremendous satisfaction as the roof of this stable gave way under the flames.

When the flames were extinguished a new life would begin.

"Now the men are gonna treat us women like ladies!"

"No more smell of cows in our underwear!"

"At last, we'll be able to buy our meat like civilized people. Buy our meat instead of killing it—and pay cash!"

The distant blazing stables looked like stars come to rest on earth. Those who had just wandered off with their animals approached respectfully. A villager held out a lighted match to J. J. Bourdage.

"Throw that in my hay so my stable'll catch on fire too. With that wind from the south it'll burn like a ten-dollar bill!"

The villager unfolded a ten-dollar bill, set fire to it and threw it into the wind that sent it off to burn in the sky. A woman paralyzed with wonder watched her stable burn; the flames were painting the walls of her house with shadows and spots of red.

"Look, it's as if my whole house had turned to gold!"

The flames swelled, trying to fly into the night. The animals that had been chased away returned to the fold.

"Only thing those goddamn animals understand is the knife!" said Arsène, opening the blade of his pocket-knife.

He approached the cow, tapped its neck.

"Poor cow, you ain't got no stable now."

He felt a familiar warmth on his hands; he had sunk the blade of his knife into the animal's neck and it was racing, head down, towards its burning stable.

"Your blood don't come out fast enough to put out the fire! " Arsène shouted.

The fire lowed like a cow and as he begged for a beer Arsène explained:

"Tomorrow morning I start digging my land underneath the barn."

"And when you find it, you can make a gold tombstone for your cow!"

The cars parked in the fields and along the main street were overflowing with coarse laughter and gentle whispers: beneath the ardour of young lovers they fluttered like toads in a trance. The radios were loud but the sweating young lovers heard only their own whispered promises.

"For the wedding I'm going to buy you a ring as big as my fist. Even the Queen of England couldn't afford a bigger one!"

On the radio the Premier was declaring:

"Under my government, which has brought prosperity, the gold will shine!"

On the radio, the Leader of the Opposition replied:

"This last-minute gold-hunt is one of the diversionary tactics the Government is using to conceal how ineffective it is in dealing with real economic problems."

In cars that were tossing with pleasure and love, lovers heard only "I love you."

"When you got gold, will you remember the good times like this?"

A young woman murmured her concern, but the young

man didn't hear her. He was thinking of tomorrow, the day when he would touch gold. Already, the young woman's body was not what he wanted to caress.

Cars were pouring along all the roads now, loaded with crying children, with men and women, their eyes bloodshot from fatigue. When they set foot in the village they weren't really strangers, so much had they dreamed about gold.

J. J. Bourdage went from one to the next, refusing to smoke with one, refusing to drink with another. He gladly offered his hand, but withdrew it when a woman tried to put it on her breast.

"How come you ain't smoking?" asked a man, insulted to see him refuse a cigar which he'd been keeping in a drawer for nine years, waiting for the right event to celebrate.

"I don't like smoke," said J. J. Bourdage. "I like solid things—like gold!"

A woman clutched his hand; the woman was an extravagant flame.

"Come in the garden with me. My husband's running after the cows and the tomatoes are high!"

"A man like me's gotta be faithful."

"I'm so glad about the gold you found I don't want to celebrate it with my husband!"

"There's lots of men around, Madame."

"I know what it is, you're scared of women."

"It's tomorrow that I'm scared of."

The night spread to the frontiers of the earth; and yet he felt closed in, as though he were in a dark cell where he had to count his steps so as not to bump into the wall. These men and women with their chubby faces looked like potatoes. But what did he look like? The potatoes they wore instead of faces belonged to them, but what face did he wear on this dark night where non-existent gold was shining? He had the undecided face of a man who is running away. He could make off with the money that belonged to these men he despised, but he could never extort a single spark of joy. The flames burning down the stables and barns had set fire to the pleasure he took from carrying out his Big Deal. He wasn't happy to see the celebration he'd been preparing for so long crackle like fire out of control. His soul rubbed against his flesh, dry as sand. The celebration had no taste. His only pleasure would come when he got into his white Cadillac. He'd go back to the Auberge du Bon Boire. Morning would come. The dancers would go to sleep. The flames would die down. Then he would go, in peace, without joy or regret. Behind a burning cherry tree, gentle sobbing. A child perhaps. Elsewhere there was laughter. And somewhere else, there was mooing. And the shrieks of cars. It didn't stop. Every celebration has its tears. He went back inside the Auberge du Bon Boire and his white hat was wet with sweat and dew. Behind the cherry tree, Ti-queue, who used to cut the bulls' cords but who had been running a bulldozer since the arrival of the graduate veterinarians, grabbed hold of a girl he'd fished out of the black waters of the night. Despite her fingernails and her shouts and the way she lashed out at him, he managed to lay her down in the grass where he held her by the wrists, arms outstretched.

"Come on, let me," Ti-queue implored. "We're rich, we got the right!"

"No! No!" cried the girl.

"If your father's pissed off I'll give him a bag of gold."

"No! I don't want to do it with you!"

"We're rich, we're laying on gold!"

"I don't want gold, I want out of here!"

J. J. Bourdage arrived at the Auberge. His white Cadillac was almost alone in the parking lot. Many of the cars that had been imprisoning his had gone. Perhaps, at last, he could . . .

"Boss! Hey, Boss!"

Someone was pulling on his arm.

"We need a judge and you're the man we want, Boss!"

He was led across from the church, on the mountaintop. In the yellowish light of the street lamps, the villagers poured towards the church. The street was empty of cars.

"We cleaned off the street because we had to," his guide explained.

The villagers stood close together in front of the church. When they saw J. J. Bourdage's white hat appear they moved aside to let him pass.

"They'll explain, Boss," said his guide, "what's gonna happen right here under our eyes in front of the church, under the good Lord's great night. Them two boys you see in the car, that's Banane Couture's son-in-law and Ovila Gornouille's son-in-law. Them two son-in-laws bought themselves new cars tonight when they found out they were rich enough to fart gold. They decided to have a contest. They're betting their new cars and their land. Both of them. The winner's gonna get real rich, but he promises to support the loser and his kids and his family. The first Friday of every month the loser's got the right to take a little shovelful of dirt from the winner."

In the distance, J. J. Bourdage thought he noticed the dawn opening its eyelids as though it were awakening. He had hoped that sleep would carry them all away before the light appeared. They'd be awake for a long time yet. Each one lingered, contemplating his concealed madness.

"So you're gonna judge the contest, eh Boss? Did you see the ox?"

Farmers placed a bull across the street, between two cars with their backs to each other. Using a rope tied to the ring in its nose, they attached it to a hydro pole. Then, tying its tail in a slip-knot, they attached the other end of the bull to another hydro pole on the other side of the street. Thus the bull blocked off the street completely. On the top of the mountain, in front of the church, the street was cut off by a bellowing wall. At the foot of the mountain, far off in the fields, was a blinking ribbon of headlights. J. J. Bourdage pushed back his hat. This gesture indicated that he was ready to begin his work as a judge. A woman took his arm in hers and squeezed against him. Her soft warmth made him shudder.

"I'll explain the rules of this here game, Boss. Right here underneath it's the very middle of the village. The official middle's right in front of the church. The two ends of the village, that's where the pavement stops on the main street. After that it's gravel. We got witnesses at both ends of the village. The cars are gonna sit with their rear ends on the gravel of the other parish at both ends of the village and their noses on our asphalt. The signal's gonna be when they hit the old church bell, the one that fell down there, with a sledge-hammer. When the bell rings Ovila Gornouille's son-in-law and Banane Couture's son-in-law mustn't think it's time for mass. They better think about getting in their cars and piling on that ox. The first car that hits the ox, that's the winner. The others one's gonna be real poor! Gotta kill the ox!"

The motors backfired. The villagers moved back. The cars backed away from the bull and headed for the village limits. They waited. The bell rang. From the depths of night you could hear the echo of roaring. The motors were enraged. From the mountaintop you could see the two cars coming closer, each one on its own side; they leaped from bump to knoll. Their headlights projected ragged beams. Suddenly thunder struck them in the face. Hot worms slithered through the villagers' hair. It was blood from the bull, which had exploded between the two cars. When they dared to open their eyes again the cars were blazing the way their church had blazed. They observed in silence. The Curé blessed the two victims. Then there was nothing left for the fire to devour, only twisted red metal. There seemed to be just one car with another one in its stomach.

"Who's the winner?"

When he heard the voice J. J. Bourdage thought he was being wrenched from a dream.

"Is it Banane Couture's son-in-law or Ovila Gornouille's?"

"Do you think," J. J. Bourdage asked, "the loser's gonna want to dig up a shovelful of dirt from the winner's land?"

"We gotta know who won the other one's gold. That's what we had the contest for."

The torn metal gave off sparks. J. J. Bourdage examined the balls of chewed-up metal. The stars in the sky reflected men's dreams.

"I'll swear on your gold that I saw the noses of both them cars touch at the same time, *at the same time*, I saw it, they touched the bull's sides."

Enthusiastic applause approved his verdict.

"When they build the church again," said Miss Catechism, "we'll put the bodies of the cars on top of the altar. They'll be beautiful, painted gold, because they'll be a modern-day crucifix."

The woman clinging to J. J. Bourdage's arm clung closer to him and he remembered that she was there.

"Boss, is it true that people that get in the habit of touching gold don't like touching women any more!"

J. J. Bourdage pulled his hat down over his eyes.

"Madame, a man's gotta choose—women or gold."

She squeezed his arm harder. He freed himself briskly.

"Living in gold, Madame, is like living in prison," he said impatiently.

He made his way through the rubbernecks gawking at the smoking debris. He left the main street, jumped over a fence between two houses and headed for the fields. There he found a quiet tree, a rock where he could wait for the village to sleep. Then he'd quietly get into his white Cadillac and no one would suspect him of running away. The grass was wet from the heavy dew. His damp trousers stuck to his legs. The ground was strewn with moss-covered stones. With the village at his back he advanced in a black sea. He was at the age when men have houses and children asleep in fragrant sheets, but here he was in a field, looking for a tree where he could hide, waiting for dawn so he could run away. And where would he go? What invisible hand had brought him here? Against the black night he could make out the pointed shape of a tall spruce tree. He refused to answer the questions the night was breathing at him. He spoke out loud to hide the persistent voice of the night that was breathing at him. He spoke out loud to hide the persistent voice of the night that was questioning him. With rhetorical flourishes he congratulated himself for the way he'd handled himself throughout his Big Deal. Luck had been on his side. Thanks, Lady Luck! Several times, he'd had to stop himself from believing his own lies. The more he talked the less he heard and the less he saw of the night. Was it time to start dreaming about his next venture? No one would ever again be able to make the farmers believe that the stones in their land were chunks of gold, but there'd always be something else to make somebody believe. He'd invent another Big Deal. Invent . . . J. J. Bourdage was alone because he invented. Others took, gathered . . . slipped away. He invented.

The ground opened up.

The night swayed. He saw the earth, very high, very far, in place of the night. He fell, slowly, very slowly, into the endless depths of the night. The night flowed over his body as though he were being buried. He had stumbled into the trench dug by Petit-Lecourt and the shoemaker, impatient to get a glimpse of their gold. The two adventurers, attracted by the noise of the festivities, had abandoned their search. J. J. Bourdage struck his head against an iron shovel and then it bounced off a stone. At his age, his thoughts were black. The flesh on his bones mimicked the earth's inertia. No light. No pain. No strength. No sorrow. No regret.

And yet, someone was breathing in the trench. A breath touched his body. A breath that couldn't be confused with the coolness coming from the earth. Feet were stepping on the damp earth. J. J. Bourdage thought it would be wise to light a match.

"Don't bother," said a small voice that was not unfamiliar. "I can see you very clearly."

J. J. Bourdage struggled to see.

"Your eyes will get used to our dark. You're new in this country, but soon you'll realize that it's no darker than the light on earth."

J. J. Bourdage had to reply to this nonsense.

"You're looking for gold?" asked the small voice. "Gold is light, isn't it? If you can't find light on earth you won't find it in the ground."

"I want to get out of here as fast as I can. Help!"

He gesticulated. He thought he was gesticulating. But he was still unmoving. The only motion came from his breathing. Slow breathing. He thought he had the strength to hoist his shoulders out of the earth and sit up: he could see! He recognized the face of the little Notary in love, who turned his back to him and went on his way. He followed the Notary like a little dog.

"A man who loves," said the little voice, "can do without gold."

"I want out."

"I love a woman and I just have to say her name and the night, young man, becomes transparent as a spring. That's the kind of gold a man spends his whole life in search of."

"Help! I'm scared of lunatics!"

The path the Notary was following was dazzlingly bright: a streak of lightning in a black luxuriance.

"It's gold! It's gold!" J. J. Bourdage exclaimed.

Would he clutch the vein of gold that resembled the brilliant root of a tree whose trunk spread so far that he couldn't see its golden leaves? The little voice ahead of him:

"Maryitsa! Maryitsa! I'd rather be dead and in love with you than alive and without love!"

J. J. Bourdage saw the Notary disappear into the shadowy foliage. He saw him disappear into the night. Sure that no one was observing him, J. J. Bourdage knelt and touched the vein of gold. It was soft. He grazed it with his lips as though it were the forehead of a child.

"Maryitsa! Maryitsa!"

Shouting the name of a woman until it echoed, listening to the name being repeated, calling to a woman as the body calls the soul, as winter calls forth spring, pronouncing the name of a woman in the vast silence and hearing all the silence drowning in the name—that was what J. J. Bourdage wanted. Violently, like thirst. His lips opened to utter a woman's name but silence froze his lips. He knew no woman's name to shout in the night, to the heavens, to the wind. He darted ahead to catch up with the Notary. But he ran into a wall of earth and stones. He collapsed, weeping, his head on a root of the golden tree whose leaves gave off millions of sparks as day drew near.

The morning was like the morning after the night when the church had been destroyed. The light contained a memory of smoke. Some villagers were about to go to their stables, but suddenly remembered they'd set fire to them. Others were sorry they'd burned their stables: they remembered seeing the flames burst out of them, but their stables were intact, among the other buildings. Cows roamed hopelessly around the houses. In the gardens were battered, overturned cars. The grass was strewn with stray articles of clothing. No gold shone in the rocky ground. Men and women shouted greetings or insults in the same voice. Children squalled. Some of the villagers didn't dare to leave their houses. Remorse kept them inside. Or a certain fear that they wouldn't encounter the dream of the previous night. The morning was the same morning that came to the village every day, but today it was appearing after a great dream. On the main street, cars they had never seen collided. Trailers were parked on the lawns. Unknown children whined as they chased one another. Unknown people walked around with shovels on their shoulders. Villagers had invaded the fields and were starting to dig.

"If we don't find gold at least our grave'll be ready!"

They dug with all their might. One day they would die; but as long as they were alive they needed gold.

J. J. Bourdage woke up. He had slept as he'd never slept before. There were bloodstains on his hands. He rushed to the mirror in his cell. A wall was in his way. A wall of earth. And a shovel leaning aginst the wall. There was blood on the shovel. Why did he imagine he was standing? He was only sitting. He got up. He saw a field and a group of houses; a village he'd never seen before. He wasn't in his cell, he was in a hole that had been dug in a field. Men with shovels seemed to be looking for something. They dug here and there. His blood-stained hands clutched the surface of the ground and his feet projected him out of the trench. His clothes were covered with mud. At the bottom of the trench he noticed a large white hat stained with mud, perhaps with blood. The men would put down their shovels and explain what was happening. What a story! Lie down in your cell and wake up in a field, free!

"Number 2786 has lost his cell, ha ha ha! Please return if you fi . . ."

He was certain he hadn't put his lips to the wood alcohol the prisoners brought back from the paint-shop. Men with shovels over their shoulders were heading towards him. All together they had stopped digging in the ground. He didn't know that his face was covered with dried blood. Why were they looking at him with such curiosity? Likely because he was a stranger.

"Where's the gold?"

"Where do we dig up the gold?"

"Did you see my cell?"

"The gold! Did you find any gold in the ground or didn't you?"

"Capital G-O-L-D."

"I didn't find any gold," J. J. Bourdage assured them.

One of the villagers raised his shovel, ready to strike.

"You goddamn thief!"

He shouted to the men who were starting to dig in the next field.

"Get over here. Looks like there ain't no gold."

J. J. Bourdage spun around and started to run. But the villagers immediately circled him and crushed him to the ground.

"Gold?" he repeated, not understanding.

The men, with their wrinkles and their beards and their teeth, looked like furious dogs. Suddenly he remembered. His memory was limpid.

"The gold! I remember! I remember!"

He no longer looked like a man who can't recognize his own face without a mirror. The villagers saw him as Monsieur Bourdage again. This night was a celebration for him too, wasn't it?

"I remember! The gold was in a book. But I can't find the goddamn book. It was in my cell. But I lost my cell!"

Something struck him in the face: a pebble, a shovel, a foot or a fist. It burned. It didn't hurt.

It was a custom in the village every autumn to watch the parade of triumphant cars bearing a corpse on their roofs, a deer or a moose. On this spring morning, the silent villagers reflected as a Cadillac drove past, bearing instead of a deer or a moose, a man, J. J. Bourdage, crucified on its roof. His blood dripped down onto the white paint.

"Gold!" the villagers demanded.

"Gold!"

"Gold!"

"There's a man that's going to keep his secret."

"It's our secret too."